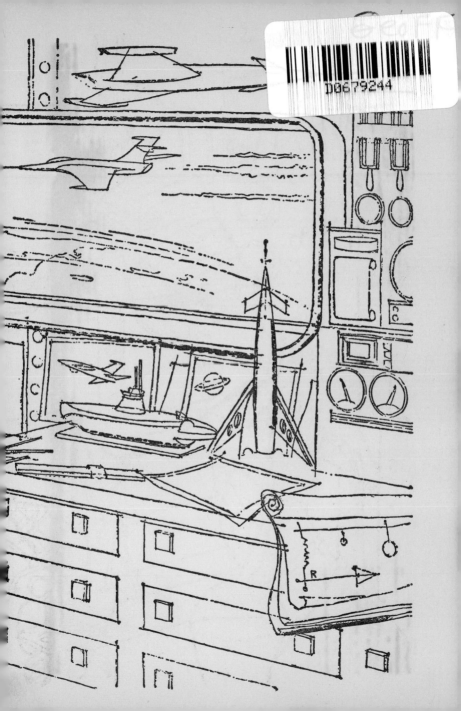

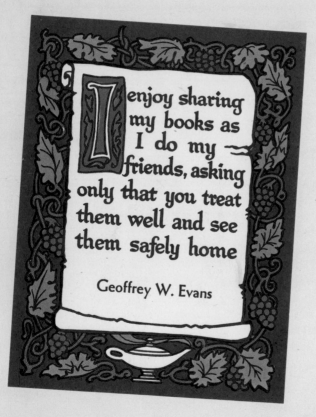

I enjoy sharing my books as I do my friends, asking only that you treat them well and see them safely home

Geoffrey W. Evans

TOM SWIFT AND HIS SONIC BOOM TRAP

A weird blast of sound engulfs an American city. Tom is caught in the panic while visiting there to demonstrate his new sonic boom deadener—the Silentenna—at a Noise Reduction Conference. A top-rank scientist, John Wyvern, who is also attending the conference, mysteriously vanishes the day of the sonic attack.

Attempts on the lives of both Tom and Wyvern's pretty daughter intensify the young inventor's determination to solve the mystery. A clue to John Wyvern's whereabouts takes Tom to the sun-scorched Australian Outback, where he uses his latest invention—a robot bloodhound—to track down the missing scientist, but a deadly bush fire wipes out the trail.

Meanwhile, other cities in the United States have suffered terrifying eruptions of sound. The President receives an unsigned ultimatum, threatening an all-out sonic blitz unless the blackmailer's price of ten million dollars is paid.

Tom's Silentenna offers the only hope of defense—but to perfect it he needs a special liquid-crystal device which only the missing scientist can supply. The young inventor's race against time to thwart the unknown sonic enemy will keep every reader's pulse pounding with excitement and suspense.

"Tom! Is this an atomic attack?" Bud yelled

TOM SWIFT

AND HIS

SONIC BOOM TRAP

BY VICTOR APPLETON II

ILLUSTRATED BY EDWARD MORITZ

GROSSET & DUNLAP

NEW YORK PUBLISHERS

CONTENTS

CHAPTER I

SECRET MESSAGE

"JUMPIN' jets! What happened?" exclaimed Bud Barclay as a loud crash resounded outside Tom Swift's private laboratory.

The clattering echoes were followed by a bellowed outburst of Texas range talk.

"Sounds like Chow!" said Tom Swift. The blond, lanky young inventor dashed from his workbench to open the door. His dark-haired friend Bud followed close behind.

As the two eighteen-year-olds peered into the corridor, they saw Chow Winkler, the Swifts' fat cowboy-cook, picking himself off the floor. His face was covered with white topping from a ruined lemon meringue pie, and the floor was strewn with broken crockery and spilled food from the lunch tray Chow had been carrying.

Nearby a strange-looking mechanical creature

was slowly and contentedly wagging its head over a puddle of hot stew.

"Git yore lowdown, clumsy carcass out o' my vittles!" Chow roared. The bald-headed chef aimed a kick at the mobile robot.

Sensing the oncoming boot by radar, the automaton hastily rolled back out of range on its rubber tractor treads. Caught off balance, Chow skidded on the slippery floor and sat down with a thud!

Bud was rocking with laughter. "Fido really has Chow frothing at the mouth!" he gasped. "This could be the first case on record of Mad Man Bites Dog!"

"Cut the wisecracks," Tom advised, "or you could be the first guy Chow ever served red-peppered food!"

The roly-poly cook had heard Bud's outburst of hilarity. Chow's white-smeared face turned redder than ever with rage when he saw the boys grinning at his predicament.

"Oh—oh! Plug your ears!" Bud said. "We're about to get blasted!"

"Quick! Inside!" Tom hissed. "I just had an idea!"

He darted to the center of the room as Bud slammed the door. An unusual-looking electronic device was mounted on the workbench. Tom barely had time to flick it on before Chow Winkler came stumping into the laboratory.

"Brand my pothooks, boss!" he stormed. "If that hydrophobiated mechanical polecat don't—"

Suddenly Chow's voice was cut off. His mouth continued moving and his jaws worked vigorously, but not a sound came from his throat!

The cook's eyes widened with panic as he tried again and again to shout at the boys. But the silence in the lab remained unbroken. Chow began to gesture frantically and clutch his neck.

Clicking a knob on the electronic device, Tom said calmly, "What's the matter, Chow? Don't be bashful. If there's something you want to tell us, please say it right out." The young inventor kept a straight face, but his eyes were twinkling.

"I—I can't talk!" Chow croaked. Hearing his own voice again, the plump Texan gave a shudder of relief.

Then he saw the grins on Tom's and Bud's faces. "Were you funnin' me jest now, boss, with some kind o' scientific hokey-pokey?" Chow asked suspiciously.

The two boys burst out laughing.

"Yes, I was, Chow," Tom confessed. "But please don't get sore. I couldn't resist the temptation to show off my latest invention."

"You mean that there thingamabob on the bench?" Chow pointed to a solid block of clear plastic which revealed the electronic circuitry inside it. A pancake-shaped metal unit was mounted on an upright support atop the plastic.

"That's right. I call it the Silentenna Mark I," said Tom. "Here, I'll show you how it works. Give us a whistle, Bud."

Bud pursed his lips and began whistling shrilly. Tom switched on his invention. As he turned a control knob, the whistle faded into silence. A reverse turn made the whistle audible again.

"You see, this transducer on top of the Silentenna emits sounds of equal frequency and volume to any sounds which the device 'hears,' " said Tom. "But the output sound waves are exactly out of phase with the input, so the incoming sounds—in this case, Bud's whistle—are canceled out."

"Wal, bake me fer a bean!" The good-natured cook was so amazed he forgot all about being angry. "That's plumb wonderful, boss!"

The young inventor shook his head. "Thanks, but I'm afraid it's not all that good, Chow." Tom explained that he was trying to perfect a "sonic boom trap" to silence the blastlike shock wave caused by aircraft flying faster than the speed of sound. "This Mark I of mine only works at short ranges," he added. "I'll have to come up with something a lot better than this."

Chow's face darkened as he remembered his recent accident. "I jest wish you'd never come up with that sneakin' varmint Fido," he complained. "The blame thing was snoozin' in the hallway, an' as I come by with that tray o' food, brand my hide if it didn't attack me an' trip me up—deliberately!"

Tom smothered a chuckle. "Sorry, old-timer. It must have sensed that hot stew you were carrying and tried to get as close to the heat as possible."

"There it is now," said Bud. "The creeping brain itself."

The odd-looking robot had rolled in through the doorway of the laboratory and was rotating its head from side to side.

"I'll make hash out o' that there robot if it don't stay out o' my way!" Chow fumed. "Lock it up somewhere, boss, while I git you buckaroos more grub."

Fido—named for Feedback Informational Deductive Organism—was a mobile adaptive machine which Tom had built to help shed light on the thinking and learning processes of living beings. It was powered by a thermionic device which converted heat directly into electricity. The automaton moved freely about the lab building, guided by infrared sensors, seeking sunshine and other sources of heat to "feed on."

Chow soon returned, this time with a lunch cart, and the two boys hungrily began eating the delicious mulligan stew.

"Are you going to show your Silentenna in Detroit at the Noise Reduction Conference?" Bud asked.

Tom nodded. "Sure, the Mark I can be a big

help in cutting down unnecessary noises, even though it's no answer to the sonic boom problem. By the way, we'll be taking off right after lunch."

Half an hour later, as the boys were freshening up in the apartment adjoining the lab, the tele-

phone rang. Tom Swift Sr. was calling from the double office which the famous father and son shared in the Main Building at Swift Enterprises.

"Just heard from your mother, Tom," the elder scientist said. "She and the girls are on their way over to the airstrip. I said we'd meet them there in ten minutes. Okay?"

"Bud and I'll be there."

The two boys carried the Silentenna outside to a company jeep and drove across the sprawling grounds of Enterprises. At this walled, four-mile-square experimental station, Tom Jr. and Sr. developed their amazing inventions.

The *Sky Queen,* a three-decker plane, had already been raised from its underground hangar and stood ready for take-off. Tom had designed the huge atomic-powered craft as a Flying Lab.

Mr. Swift, tall and athletic-looking with graying, close-cropped hair, greeted the boys as they carried Tom's device aboard. Mrs. Swift, a slender, sweet-faced woman, arrived by car soon afterward with Tom's blond, teen-age sister Sandra and her close friend Phyllis Newton. Phyl, a brown-eyed brunette, was the daughter of Tom Sr.'s old friend, Ned Newton, who managed the Swift Construction Company. She and Sandy often double-dated Tom and Bud.

In a few minutes the sleek silver sky giant roared upward on its jet lifters. Then Tom sent it streaking westward toward the Great Lakes. Bud, a husky young flier and astronaut from California, was copilot.

Sandy and Phyl came forward to the flight compartment. Phyl smiled, saying, "What a break for us having you and your dad invite us to the convention, Tom. Three whole days—and I've never been to Detroit before!"

Sandy giggled. "Of course, you boys may not see much of us at the scientific sessions. We might have to kidnap them, Phyl, if we need escorts to show us around town."

Bud winked at Tom. "How about it, pal?" Tom grinned and nodded.

Twenty minutes later the supersonic jet was swooping down toward Detroit's Metropolitan Airport. From here, the group taxied by express-way to a hotel overlooking Grand Circus Park.

Upon entering the hotel lobby Tom and his father recognized several scientists who had come to attend the conference. One was John Wyvern, a top-rank crystallographer from the Sonicon Re-search Institute.

"That's exciting work you're doing, John, on obtaining a piezoelectric effect from supersmectic liquid crystals," Mr. Swift said as they shook hands. "I hope we'll hear more about it at these meetings."

"You will, indeed. I'm reading a paper on my latest experiments at the morning session tomor-row." Wyvern hastily introduced his attractive, twenty-one-year-old daughter, Elsa. She was soon chatting enthusiastically with Sandy and Phyl.

Wyvern, thin and sandy-haired, had a nervous, intense look. He drew aside from the others and jotted something on a slip of notepaper. As the group parted in the lobby, Wyvern slipped the note into Tom's hand.

Tom did not read it until he and Bud were in their hotel room. His forehead wrinkled.

"Hmm. That's strange," he muttered.

"What's up, genius boy?" Bud asked.

"Take a look." Tom handed him the note.

Bud read it and was as puzzled as Tom. The message from Wyvern began: *Have urgent matter to discuss with you.* It asked Tom to meet him as soon as possible at a certain coffee shop on Woodward Avenue.

"Any idea what's on his mind?" Bud asked.

Tom shook his head. "Not a clue." Picking up the telephone, Tom tried to call Wyvern's room but got no answer. "Bud, this may be important," he said. "Want to tag along?"

"Sure, if you think Wyvern won't object."

The two boys caught a taxi outside the hotel. Tom was still frowning thoughtfully as the cab sped northward from the park.

Suddenly a shrill blast of sound split the air. The taxi driver was so startled that he almost swerved into another car.

"What's *that?*" Bud asked, yelling to make himself heard. "Some sort of alarm siren?"

The driver shrugged. "It sure don't sound like any siren *I* ever heard!"

The noise grew louder and louder until the explosion of sound was almost skull-bursting!

Many cars pulled over to the curb. Tom ordered their driver to do so, too. Other cars speeded up wildly, as if the noise were an alarm signal of danger.

The blasting sound began to rise and fall crazily in pitch. Pedestrians scurried into buildings and doorways, clutching their ears. Bud, white-faced with fear, turned to his pal.

"Tom!" he shrieked. *"Can this be a warning of an atomic attack?"*

CHAPTER II

A SONIC MYSTERY

TOM shook his head uncertainly and yelled, "I doubt it—but let's find out!" He had noticed that the taxi was equipped with a radio.

"Turn on a local station!" Tom shouted to the driver. "There may be an announcement!"

The man obeyed with trembling fingers. Tom and Bud leaned forward to hear as the radio warmed up. A faintly audible crash outside drew their attention to the street. Two speeding cars had just sideswiped each other.

Brakes screeched and another crash could be heard as cars began to jam up behind the two vehicles. Horns honked vainly above the din. After a wild exchange of shouts and gestures, the two panicky motorists sped on.

Meanwhile, the driver had turned the radio on to full volume. A dance band was playing. The music was cut short by the excited voice of an announcer:

"Your attention, please! This is a special bulletin! Civil Defense officials say that the sounds being heard throughout the city are *not* sirens to warn of an emergency! Repeat—there is *no* emergency! So far, police have been unable to locate the source of the sounds, but Commissioner Johnson promises speedy action. Meantime, he begs citizens not to panic! Repeat—*do not panic!*"

The taxi driver turned a frightened face to the boys and yelled, "Don't panic, he says! Whadda we supposed to do? Plug our ears and go nuts?"

Bud grinned wryly. His own face was looking strained. Even with the taxi windows closed, the din was deafening. Both boys' heads were throbbing from the torrent of sound, and the weird undulations in pitch made it even more nerveracking.

Pedestrians were running for cover in evident terror. A bulging-eyed woman opened her mouth in an unheard scream, then collapsed on the sidewalk. A man helped her to her feet, then into a store.

Tom tried to shut out the noise by focusing his mind on the problem of who or what might be causing the devilish outburst. He racked his brain but could think of no answer.

"How much longer can this go on?" Tom wondered desperately. Perhaps he should return to the hotel at once and check on the safety of his parents, Sandy, and Phyl. But one glance at the wildly disordered traffic and the frantic drivers speeding past convinced Tom that it would be wiser to stay calmly where he was.

Suddenly the shrieking sounds began to diminish. They faded to a wail and died out. Tom and Bud looked at each other in relief and warily removed their hands from their ears.

"Whew!" Bud shook his head. "My ears are still ringing!"

"Same here," put in the driver. "My head feels half busted!"

As they drove on to the restaurant, news flashes over the radio reported numerous traffic accidents and cases of people who had collapsed during the eruption of sound.

The boys were startled by the wail of a siren. As the taxi driver pulled over, an ambulance rushed past.

"There must have been a *lot* of people who couldn't take it!" Bud commented.

"No wonder," Tom replied. "Another half hour or so of that could panic a whole city."

Arriving at the restaurant, the boys paid their driver and went inside. There was no sign of John Wyvern, so Tom and Bud sat down in a booth and ordered coffee while they waited.

"I'd like to call the hotel just to make sure everyone's okay," Tom remarked.

"Good idea," said Bud. "There's a booth over by the cashier's counter."

Tom soon managed to contact his father and learned that his group was safe. Mr. Swift was as puzzled as Tom by the strange phenomenon.

"I can't imagine what caused the sounds," the scientist said, "but they definitely weren't from ordinary sirens. If practical jokers were responsible, they should be punished—there must have been a large toll in accidents."

"There was, according to the radio news flashes," Tom said. "Not to mention all the damage to people's nervous systems!"

After hanging up, Tom rejoined Bud. The boys waited an hour, but Wyvern did not appear.

"You don't suppose he got involved in an accident on the way here, do you?" said Bud.

Tom shrugged worriedly. "Maybe I'd better check with his daughter."

Tom called the hotel again but was told that Elsa Wyvern had gone out. There was no answer from Wyvern's room. Tom had the crystallographer paged without success, then spoke to the convention registrar at the hotel, but he had no information of the scientist's whereabouts.

Alarmed, Tom telephoned police headquarters. A sergeant told him no accident had been reported involving a man answering John Wyvern's description.

It was past five o'clock before Tom was able to

reach Elsa Wyvern. She had just returned from a late shopping tour with Sandy and Phyl.

"I haven't seen Dad," Elsa answered Tom. "He told me he was going out soon after we met you folks. Oh, goodness! Do you suppose something has happened to him?"

Tom tried to reassure her and added, "Ask my father to help you search for him, Elsa. He'll know what to do."

The boys stayed at the restaurant, hoping Wyvern might still come. At a quarter to six they ordered dinner. The scientist had not appeared by the time they finished eating, so Tom and Bud returned to the hotel.

The opening session of the Noise Reduction Conference was scheduled for eight o'clock that evening. But the hotel reception room was already crowded when the two boys arrived. Tom spotted his father talking to a balding, thickset man with horn-rimmed glasses.

Mr. Swift broke off as the boys hurried toward him. "Glad you're back, son. . . . You and Dr. Kimer have met, of course. And this young fellow is one of our test pilots, Bud Barclay."

The three shook hands. Tom had already recognized the man as Dr. Olaf Kimer, the brilliant head of the Sonicon Research Institute. Kimer's pale-gray eyes stared intently at Tom through his thick-lensed spectacles.

"I understand you were to meet John Wyvern."

"Yes, but he never kept the appointment," Tom said. "Any word from him, Dad?"

"Not yet. Elsa's going to notify the police if he's not here by eight. I was hoping Dr. Kimer might know something of his whereabouts."

Kimer shook his head. "Unfortunately I don't —and I'm getting rather worried. Have you any idea what he wanted to see you about, Tom?"

"No, but I have a feeling it was something important," the young inventor replied.

As the Swifts and Bud chatted with Dr. Kimer, they were joined by two associates of Kimer at Sonicon—Victor Fronz and Arthur Gammon.

Fronz, an untidy man with a thick mop of dark hair, gave Tom a look of keen interest. "The program notes say you've been working on a sonic boom trap," he remarked.

"That's right," said Tom, "but my invention hasn't tested out too well so far."

"Are you going to demonstrate it here?" asked Gammon, a tall man with silver-gray hair.

"Yes, on Friday afternoon." Tom added, "Are you two working in the same field as Dr. Kimer?"

"Not exactly," said Gammon. "We're electronic engineers. Of course we help to rig up most of the equipment he uses."

Just then the conference public relations officer

brought over a group of reporters. They pounced on the Swifts eagerly.

"You two are up on all the latest scientific marvels," one newsman said. "What's behind these weird noises that hit Detroit today?"

"I'm afraid I don't know any more about it than you do, gentlemen," said Mr. Swift.

"That goes double," Tom added with a smile.

"Sure it wasn't some far-out publicity gag to ballyhoo this conference?"

The public relations man denied this firmly.

"Dr. Kimer, you've been working on the effects of noise stress on humans and animals," said another reporter. "What's your opinion?"

Kimer gave a shrug. "Noise can be painful, damaging—and very dangerous when it strikes a whole city as happened today. But as to the source of the sounds, I must admit I'm baffled."

"The answer to the mystery may be even stranger than you think, gentlemen," a rasping voice spoke up loudly. "Has it occurred to you that what happened today may be a *sonic invasion* by some unseen enemy?"

CHAPTER III

AN URGENT SUMMONS

EVERYONE turned to the speaker in surprise. He was a wispy man with a large beaked nose. His sallow skin was shrunken tightly over his face, giving it a skull-like appearance, but his eyes glittered brilliantly.

"Who's that?" Bud whispered to Tom.

"Search me." Tom frowned. "I'm sure I've seen him at other scientific conferences."

The reporters began hurling questions.

"What do you mean by an 'unseen enemy'?"

"And what's a 'sonic invasion'?" another newsman added.

"Perhaps you'd prefer the term 'sonic attack,' " the speaker replied. "What happened certainly amounts to an attack on this city—and a very dangerous attack—as Dr. Kimer has just told you."

"You're twisting my words, sir!" Dr. Kimer stared at the man with a puzzled frown.

"Would you mind telling us who you are?" a reporter asked the beak-nosed man.

"My name, gentlemen, is Phineas Gull."

"Mr. Gull is a science-fiction writer," the public relations officer put in hastily, looking somewhat embarrassed.

Some of the reporters grinned. One muttered, "No wonder!"

But the first newsman who had spoken seemed to scent a good feature story. "You still haven't told us what you meant by an 'unseen enemy,' " he said.

"It's obvious that the blast of sound which disrupted the city was not a friendly act. I submit that there may be enemy agents at large in the city at this very moment."

Even the grinning reporters were startled.

"Are you trying to tell us the sounds were a hostile act—maybe an act of war—by some unknown enemy invaders?" the newsman persisted.

Phineas Gull smiled mysteriously. "Merely suggesting an answer which fits the facts."

"You're dodging the question," another reporter spoke up. "Do *you* think that's the answer?"

"Find the source of those sounds or offer a better explanation, and I'll withdraw what I just said," Gull replied. "Had the sounds continued, the whole city could have been thrown into chaos. Dr. Kimer can tell you all about the physical and mental damage caused by prolonged noise stress."

By now the reporters were scribbling furiously. The beak-nosed science fictioneer was clearly enjoying the spotlight. He droned on in his nasal voice, and seemed well versed in technical data.

Tom listened with interest. Although Gull's idea seemed too fantastic to take seriously, Tom liked to keep an open mind. But he wondered how Gull thought the "invaders" could have concealed the necessary sound-emitting equipment from notice during the attack—and why they should cease their blitz after successfully taking the city by surprise.

"I'd like to hear how you think the sounds were generated," Tom put in quietly, "and why they *didn't* continue longer."

Gull's glittering eyes darted toward Tom.

"Gentlemen, I'm amazed that our teen-aged scientific genius should be stumped by such a simple problem," he sneered. "*I* can outline half a dozen ways in which the sounds could have been generated."

Bud sizzled at Gull's rudeness. "Why, that crazy loon! Implying that you're asking him for an ABC course on sound transducers! Tom, why don't you—"

"Relax," Tom whispered. "He probably thought I was trying to needle him. Let him talk."

Gull went on lecturing to his avid audience until the conference was called to order. Later, after the evening session was over, Tom and Bud met Sandy in the hotel elevator.

"Elsa's father still hasn't shown up," she said. "I hope the police can find him!"

But next morning there was still no word on the missing crystallographer.

At breakfast Bud passed on some other news to Tom. "Wait'll you hear what a reporter told me," he said with a chuckle. "You know that loud-mouth who was sounding off last night?"

"Phineas Gull?"

"Yes. The police read about it and picked him up for questioning. But they decided he was just a nut and let him go."

John Wyvern did not appear at the Noise Reduction Conference that day or the following one. On Friday, at the last session, Tom prepared to show his Silentenna Mark I. The audience took their places, eager to witness the demonstration.

"The effective range of my Silentenna is too limited for it to serve as a sonic boom trap," Tom told the assembled scientists. "But as you know, there's an urgent need to reduce the noise level in modern cities and factories—and my invention should be effective for this use. I suggest you all start talking at once. Then, as I switch on the power, you will observe its silencing effect."

Soon the meeting room hummed with loud chatter. Tom clicked a knob on the clear plastic unit and turned up the volume control.

Nothing happened!

The audience was puzzled. Their talk began to die down. Tom was red-faced.

"Most amazing," drawled a nasal voice from the front row. "A nonsilencing Silentenna!"

Bud threw a furious glance at the speaker—Phineas Gull! The young copilot clenched his fists as the man made other loud wisecracks.

"I don't need to tell you my device isn't working," Tom confessed to his listeners. He frantically checked over his invention. Suddenly he plucked several small slabs from a receptacle at the top of the plastic block.

"Here's the answer," Tom announced lamely. "Someone has substituted dummies for the oscillator crystals. Ladies and gentlemen, I'm afraid I must call off this demonstration."

The other scientists were as embarrassed as Tom. The chairman arose and said, "Knowing Tom Swift Jr. as we all do, I'm sure our opinion of his latest invention won't be affected by this unfortunate—er—mishap."

Mr. Swift joined the boys outside the meeting room. "Any idea how this happened, son?"

Tom gave an unhappy shrug. "I brought the Silentenna to the hotel from the *Sky Queen* this morning—and it was working then," he said. "It was in Bud's and my room, so the substitution must have been made there."

The hotel detective called the police. "You

should have kept your invention in our safe," he told Tom.

"I saw no reason to. The device isn't secret—it'll be available to any manufacturer."

The police checked the boys' room for prints and questioned the hotel staff but could find no clues.

That evening Elsa Wyvern dined with the Swifts but could eat little. The pretty, red-haired girl still had had no word of her father.

Mrs. Swift said kindly, "It'll be dreadful for you, waiting here alone in a strange city. Why not come back to Shopton with us until the police have something to report?"

"We'd love having you!" Sandy urged.

Elsa's eyes filled with tears. "Thank you. I can't think of anything I'd rather do."

It was dusk when the *Sky Queen* took off and winged eastward across Lake Erie. Tom had just finished talking to an FAA Flight Service Station when a burst of static came over the radio. A faint voice filtered through the static:

"This is John Wyvern calling Tom Swift!"

The young inventor and Bud were electrified at hearing the missing scientist's name.

"Tom here! Come in, please! Where are you?"

The voice named a lonely wilderness area in upper New York State and went on, "Please come and pick me up as quickly as possible!"

"Someone has substituted dummies for the oscillator crystals!" Tom said lamely

Tom hastily summoned Elsa and Mr. Swift, then said, "What's going on? Why did you disappear?"

The static became worse for a moment. The voice finally came through again, saying, "I can't explain now, but my life is in danger!"

As Mr. Swift and Elsa came into the flight compartment, Tom hurriedly explained the situation.

Elsa gave a gasp of excitement. "Dad, this is Elsa!" she exclaimed over the radio. "Please tell us what this is all about!"

"I can't! Not now, Carrottop! Just trust me—and please tell Tom to do as I say!"

Tom whispered, "He wants me to land and pick him up. But there may be something fishy about all this. With all that static, how can you be sure it's his voice?"

"It must be! No one but Dad ever calls me 'Carrottop'! Please pick him up!" Elsa begged.

Tom glanced at his father, who gave a worried nod. "Give us exact directions, please," the young inventor spoke into the mike.

The voice did so. "I'll mark a landing spot with flares," it added.

In minutes the *Queen* had streaked to the spot —a flat, barren cliff top backed by a wooded ridge. Burning flares pinpointed a suitable landing position in the darkness.

Tom switched on his father's latest giant searchlight. It lit up the ground with sunlike brilliance. No figure was visible below.

"Must be hiding in the timber," Bud said.

The Flying Lab began to descend. *BOOM!* A terrific blast below suddenly shook the area!

CHAPTER IV

A DROPPED WATCH

THE *Sky Queen* shuddered in the shock waves from the explosion. Elsa and Mr. Swift were thrown against the compartment bulkhead.

Tom fought the controls. As he gunned the jet lifters, the huge craft zoomed upward.

"Look!" Bud gasped, pointing below.

A large section of the cliff had been ripped out by the blast. Stones and debris were pouring down the hillside.

"Good night!" Tom murmured in awe. "We'd have been flown to bits if we'd landed!"

After steadying Elsa, Mr. Swift gazed down at the scene. "The radio call was a trick to ambush us," he said grimly. "There must have been a bomb planted in the brush."

"Right, Dad. The exhaust heat from our jet lifters must have detonated it too soon!"

Over the intercom Tom reassured the others

28

aboard and ordered his flight engineer to check for damage. Meanwhile, he skimmed back and forth over the ridge, raking the woods with the *Queen's* powerful searchlight.

"Fat chance of spotting anyone in all that forest!" Bud observed gloomily.

"I can't believe Dad would do such a thing," Elsa sobbed.

"Don't worry, my dear," Mr. Swift soothed her. "None of us believes *now* that it was your father's voice we heard. Suppose we go back and join my wife and the girls."

The flight engineer soon reported that the Flying Lab's powerful structure appeared undamaged. Tom radioed a full report to the FAA Traffic Control Center and was told that the FBI and State Police would be notified.

"Roger! We're continuing on to Shopton."

Next morning at the experimental plant the Swifts discussed the bombing with Harlan Ames, Enterprises' dark, lean-jawed security chief.

"You're sure Wyvern himself wasn't behind this?" Ames asked.

Mr. Swift shook his head. "I find such an idea unthinkable. John Wyvern is a scientist with the highest principles."

"I agree," Tom said. "In any case, he surely wouldn't have hatched such a plot with his own daughter aboard the *Queen*."

"Then how did the man whose voice you heard

know Wyvern's pet name for Elsa?" Ames went on.

"That part stumps me," Tom admitted, "unless Wyvern has been kidnapped and his captors forced the information out of him."

"Do you think all this had any connection with the sabotage of your Silentenna?"

Tom ran his fingers through his blond crew cut. "You've got me, Harlan. Luckily, the theft of the crystals isn't important. Besides, I have an idea for a brand-new type of Silentenna. I'll start work on it right away."

"Well, I'll follow through with the FBI," Ames promised. "By the way, even though your demonstration flopped, it stirred up a lot of interest. There have already been four different phone calls this morning from newsmen and magazine writers wanting to see what you two are cooking up these days at Enterprises."

Tom and his father exchanged harried grins. Hardly a month went by without a conducted press tour of the vast experimental station. Now there would have to be another.

"Set one up for next Wednesday, Harlan," said Mr. Swift.

Tom was eager to explore a new principle for blanking out sound waves and was soon deep in experiments to devise a Silentenna Mark II. Over the weekend, he and Bud took the three girls out to dinner and a movie. But on Monday the young inventor plunged back to work in his laboratory.

On Wednesday morning Bud dropped into the lab. "Did you see who's giving the place the once-over?" he asked.

"In the press group?" Tom said. "Not yet."

"One of them's our old pal, Phineas Gull!"

Tom looked up in surprise. Then he grinned. "Well, as a science-fiction writer, I guess he has as much right to apply for the tour as anyone else. Bud, I think we should do our bit to make sure his visit isn't wasted. Let's find Arv."

Arvid Hanson, a burly but delicate-fingered craftsman who often built Tom's pilot models, had been detailed to conduct the tour. Later, when Tom and Bud arrived, he turned the group over to Tom.

The young inventor showed them his lab but neatly ducked Phineas Gull's mocking questions about his work on a new-model Silentenna. The newsmen were intrigued with Fido, especially when they saw how the robot would dart hungrily toward the heat of a lighted match, like a dog responding to a dinner whistle.

Tom explained how Fido had "learned" the best places in the building to probe for heat energy at different times of day. When his batteries were fully charged, the robot would "sleep" or "play" friskily about the corridors, but would start prowling hungrily when its supply of electricity began running down.

Gull's lip curled scornfully. "This is nothing new," he sneered. "I'd say Gray Walter's machines in England and 'the Beast' at the Johns Hopkins Applied Physics Lab are far more advanced and instructive."

"Those are outstanding projects," Tom agreed, "but I hope Fido may offer some new angles on memory and learning."

Once more Gull began to show off his knowledge. Tom let him talk. The other press visitors looked bored as Gull droned on.

Tom led the group out to the airfield. He paused near a jet plane. Around its needle nose was mounted an odd-looking ring.

"Maybe these gentlemen would be interested in hearing your theories about that blitz of sound in Detroit, Mr. Gull," Tom said.

Several newsmen groaned. Annoyed, Gull replied, "Maybe they'd rather hear why your so-called Silentenna failed to do any silencing!"

"The oscillator crystals had been removed," Tom said. "But if you think my invention wouldn't have worked, perhaps you could advise me on a better approach to the problem."

"Gladly!" Gull snapped. His eyes took on a malicious gleam—but as he began speaking, no sounds came from his mouth!

"Hmm. That's very interesting," said Tom, pretending that he was listening intently.

Gull's jaws worked frantically. Tom pretended

not to notice anything amiss. "I'll certainly make a note of that," he murmured.

The reporters began to grin, sensing that the young inventor was having some fun at the expense of his unpleasant guest. As Tom gestured with his finger, Gull's voice suddenly came through.

"Help me!" he choked. "Do something!"

"I'm sorry," Tom said apologetically. "There's nothing wrong with your voice. I just wanted to show you my Silentenna does work quite well, even though its range is limited."

"Your S-Silentenna?" Gull spluttered.

Tom nodded and pointed toward the jet plane. Bud appeared in the cabin window, grinning and holding up a clear plastic block.

"That ring around the nose of the plane is a transducer device for sonic boom tests," Tom explained. "The Silentenna circuitry is encased in that plastic block. My assistant simply turned it on and off to silence your voice."

The newsmen burst into howls of laughter.

"Still want to tell Tom Swift how to redesign his Silentenna?" one gibed at Gull.

The science-fiction writer was shaking with rage. "Go ahead and laugh, you apes!" he snarled. "As for you, Swift—you'll regret this!"

Gull stalked off toward the main gate.

Shortly after lunch Tom received a call from the airfield tower. "A plane belonging to Dr. Olaf

Kimer requests permission to land," the controller reported. "Says he flew here to visit you, skipper."

Tom readily okayed the landing. Minutes later, he greeted Dr. Kimer in his laboratory.

"Dad will be sorry he missed you," Tom said. "He had to hop over to our rocket base on Fearing Island."

"No matter." Kimer took some papers from his briefcase. "These may interest you and your father. They're reports from hospitals in Detroit on the victims of that sound outrage."

Tom glanced at them. "Anything unusual?"

"Several suffered brain damage. Two others almost died from shock reaction."

Tom gave a whistle. "Good grief! I had no idea the effects were that serious."

"It's not surprising," said Dr. Kimer. "Experiments at Bellevue Hospital in New York have shown that sudden noise can raise the brain pressure far above normal. And a British Army surgeon has reported that men were actually killed in World War II by the shock effect of sound waves from explosions."

"Dad and I must read these reports."

Kimer fingered his horn-rimmed spectacles thoughtfully. "What I came to ask," he said, "is whether you've planned any experiments to test the psychological and physiological effects of your Silentenna on humans or animals?"

"No, but it's an intriguing suggestion."

"I should be most interested to learn whether the effects may be any different from a simple absence of noise—as, say, in an anechoic chamber," the scientist explained.

Tom agreed to have some experiments carried out by Enterprises' medical staff.

"By the way," Kimer asked as he prepared to leave, "how is Elsa Wyvern bearing up over her father's disappearance?"

"Fairly well. But naturally she's very worried."

"No wonder." Kimer's eyes narrowed behind their thick-lensed spectacles. "Between the two of us, Wyvern had been acting oddly for some time before the conference. I suspect he had some private worry on his mind."

Tom pondered Dr. Kimer's words as he continued his lab work that afternoon. Just before closing time Phil Radnor—Ames's blond, muscular assistant—dropped in and showed the young inventor a gold pocket watch.

"What's this, Rad?" Tom asked.

"Take a look at the back, skipper."

Tom turned the watch over and gasped. Engraved on the back of the case was the name *John Wyvern*.

"Where'd this come from?" he asked.

"A guard found it outside your lab and turned it in to 'Lost and Found,'" Radnor replied. "I've heard about Wyvern's disappearance, so I thought you'd better see it."

Tom thought for a moment. "I wonder if Dr. Kimer could have dropped it," he mused.

Picking up the phone, Tom placed a call to the Sonicon Research Institute at Crestmont, sixty miles northeast of Shopton. "This is Tom Swift calling," he told the operator who answered. "Has Dr. Kimer returned yet?"

"Just a moment, sir. I'll see."

Kimer's voice came on the line. Tom asked about the watch. Kimer sounded puzzled as he assured the young inventor he had no idea how the watch had turned up at Enterprises.

Tom hung up, frowning. "No luck. . . . Rad, I can't figure this out."

"Do you suppose it could have been dropped by someone on that press tour?" Radnor asked.

"Good question." Tom thought of Phineas Gull.

Suddenly the young inventor's eyes widened with excitement. A strange idea had just occurred to him!

CHAPTER V

ELECTRONIC SHADOW

"WHAT'S up, skipper?" Phil Radnor queried, seeing Tom's expression. "A clue?"

"I was wondering if Wyvern might have been in that group of newsmen—in disguise."

Radnor stared in amazement. "Why would he pull a stunt like that?"

"I can't even guess, Rad, unless he had some sort of breakdown or mental lapse."

The security man shook his head doubtfully. "I don't see how he could have come in under a phony name—Harlan Ames personally checked out all the visitors. But let's make sure."

Tom accompanied Radnor in a jeep to the security office. Ames, who had met Wyvern, listened to Tom's idea with a frown.

"I'd say it's out of the question, skipper, since I know most of those reporters and magazine writers. I'll double-check, though."

"Okay, do that, Harlan. I'll show the watch to Elsa and see if it's really her father's."

Tom drove home that evening in his racy-looking silver sports car. Sandy and Elsa were helping Mrs. Swift prepare dinner. Tom took out the gold watch.

"Elsa, do you recognize this?" he asked.

The red-haired girl gasped. "Why, that—that's Dad's, isn't it?" She turned the watch over and saw the name engraved on the back. "It *is!* Tom, where did you get this?"

"It was found at the plant this afternoon, near my lab," Tom replied. "Do you know whether your father had it with him in Detroit?"

"Yes, I'm positive he did!"

"Did he wear it on a chain?"

"No, just loose in his pocket—he was quite careless with it." Elsa's vivid green eyes grew big with hope and puzzlement. "But how did it get to Swift Enterprises? Could Dad have been there today?"

"It doesn't seem likely," Tom said.

Mrs. Swift had come in from the kitchen. "Can you even be sure the watch was dropped there today, son?" she said. "It might have been lying there unnoticed for some time."

"Someone must have wound it recently," Sandy put in. "It's still going. But it has a peculiar tick."

At his sister's words, Tom suddenly went white. "Give me that thing—pronto!"

Snatching the watch from Sandy, he dashed

through the kitchen and out the back door. "Don't follow me!" Tom yelled. "This is dangerous!"

Minutes later he came into the house, looking pale and shaken. "All clear," the young inventor mumbled, summoning a limp smile.

Sandy stared at her brother in horror. "Tom!" she gasped. "Y-y-you don't mean that watch was set to explode somehow?"

Tom nodded wryly. "There was a miniature but highly explosive bomb device inside," he explained. "I disarmed it."

Elsa was stunned. Tom called Enterprises' Security and arranged to have the watch taken to the FBI for examination.

Everyone was upset. When Mr. Swift returned from Fearing Island later that evening, his steel-blue eyes blazed when he heard about the fiendish trick.

"It could have been meant to kill me or Elsa—or both of us," Tom pointed out. "Whoever planted the watch may have counted on my bringing it home and giving it to her."

"Yes," the elder scientist said thoughtfully. "Elsa was also aboard the *Sky Queen* during the earlier bomb attempt. Tom, your life and mine have often been in danger from spies and other enemies—but why should anyone want to harm *her*?"

"I don't know, Dad." Tom frowned. "Unless Elsa knows something about her father's disap-

pearance—something she doesn't even realize—
that might reveal the guilt of whoever is behind
Wyvern's disappearance."

The following morning Harlan Ames came into
Tom's laboratory and informed him that, so far,
the FBI experts had been unable to glean any
clues from the watch. He himself had checked the
identity of every person in the press tour and none
of them could have been John Wyvern in
disguise.

"But I did learn one thing from the FBI that
may tie in, skipper," Ames went on. "Ever hear of
a biochemist named Truxton—or a State Department official named Gerald Hill?"

"Those names sound familiar," Tom replied
thoughtfully. "Wait a minute—didn't they disappear a year or two ago?"

"Right," said Ames. "Both were missing for a
while, but turned up a few months later. Apparently they'd suffered amnesia. Neither had any
recollection of where he had been."

Tom stared at Ames keenly. "So—?"

"I found out there have been other cases, too—
but they were hushed up, and our Intelligence
Department says the same thing has happened in
other countries—a key scientist or industrial re-
searcher or government figure disappears, then
turns up a while later with his memory a blank."

"Amnesia cases happen all the time, Harlan."

"True, and that's why nobody's jumping to any

"Don't follow me!" Tom yelled. "This is dangerous!"

conclusions," Ames replied. "But these cases seem to fit a pattern. Both the FBI and Central Intelligence are worried."

"Meaning that the people who ducked out defected to an unfriendly power—or were kidnapped?"

The security chief shrugged. "Your guess is as good as mine."

Tom was silent a moment, then said, "I sure can't believe John Wyvern is a traitor. "If his disappearance *is* part of some bigger plot, my guess is he was kidnapped. Maybe he had a hunch he was in danger, and that's why he wanted to talk to me."

The young inventor paced about restlessly. "Harlan, this makes me feel more than ever that Elsa Wyvern may be in danger, too. Don't ask me why—perhaps the kidnappers are afraid she'll wreck their scheme somehow."

"Yes, and from what has happened, I'd say you yourself rate pretty high as a target, Tom," Ames said dryly.

"Dad and I expect that sort of thing," Tom replied, "but Elsa is here as our guest and we owe her every possible protection." Suddenly a twinkle came into his eyes. "You know, Harlan, I think I can provide Elsa with round-the-clock protection."

On Friday, while Sandy, Elsa, and Phyl Newton

were having lunch at a department store, a lanky youth with crew-cut blond hair strode up to their table.

"Tom!" Phyl exclaimed, smiling happily.

"Mind if I join you?" he asked.

"Be our guest, brother dear," said Sandy in a joking voice. "Jeepers! Don't tell me you tore yourself away from your lab for little old us?"

Tom grinned. "Mother said I'd find you here. I have a little item to deliver to Elsa."

He plucked a tiny box from his pocket and handed it to her. Surprised, Elsa opened the box and took out a green cameo ring.

"How beautiful!" she gasped. "Is this for me?"

"Sure. Try it on."

The ring fit perfectly. As Elsa thanked Tom and displayed it to the other two girls, Phyl threw him a mischievous glance.

"Meanie! I think you're trying to make me jealous!" she teased. "Don't Sandy and I get anything?"

Tom chuckled. "Sure—a free lunch, so order a big meal!"

Sandy scented a mystery behind her brother's gift and nagged him with questions, but Tom evaded them jokingly.

As they left the tearoom, Phyl said, "We're going to the beach in my convertible. Can you take the afternoon off and come with us?"

"Thanks, I'd like to but I must get back to the plant," Tom said. "I'll walk with you to the parking lot, though."

None of the three girls noticed Tom wink and signal to someone when they came out of the store. The girls' faces grew puzzled as they walked along the street.

"Is there something funny about us—or am I just imagining things?" said Sandy.

"That's what I was wondering," Elsa murmured. "Why is everyone staring at us?"

A grin twitched at Tom's lips. "Take a look behind you," he advised.

Elsa turned and her eyes widened in amazement. "Good grief!" she exclaimed. "What's that?"

"Your new electronic watchdog," said Tom.

CHAPTER VI

CALLING OUTER SPACE!

"MY new watchdog?" Elsa gasped, looking at the strange creature that had been rolling along behind them. It stopped obediently as Tom and the girls paused on the sidewalk.

The thing had a ferocious bulldog face, pricked-up bat ears, and big, round glass eyes. Its neck was circled by a crystal-studded collar and its body was mounted on caterpillar treads.

"A dog robot!" Phyl cried delightedly.

"Tom! That isn't Fido, is it?" Sandy asked.

"You've guessed it. Fido with a new head—plus a few other changes." Tom explained that instead of seeking out heat energy to generate electricity as it had done in the lab, the device was now powered by a Swift solar-charged battery.

"But where did it come from?" asked Elsa, bewildered.

Tom gestured with a grin toward the traffic in

the street. Bud, cruising slowly past in a panel truck, waved and whistled.

"He turned Fido loose on the pavement when he saw us come out of the store," Tom replied. "After that, Fido simply homed on a radio beam from a tiny transmitter in your ring. His ears are really small directional dish antennas to pick up your signal."

"So that's why you presented me with this lovely cameo!" Elsa smiled.

"Right. From now on, you'll have a hard time getting away from Fido—he'll never let you out of his sight. But if you do want to park him for a while," Tom added, "just twist his nose. It's a shutoff switch."

Elsa smiled, but then gave the young inventor a troubled glance. "I'm still not sure *why* you designed him to trail me around all the time."

Tom hesitated, not wanting to alarm Elsa. "Maybe I'm a worrywart," he said, "but after that watch business, I decided to try to protect you from danger. If anyone bothers you, just press that stone in your ring and he'll take over from there."

"I think he's cute!" Phyl said admiringly.

"So do I," Elsa said, patting the automaton's bulldog head. "Thanks a million, Tom, for giving me such a loyal protector."

Sandy chuckled. "He won't take a blue ribbon at a dog show, but I'm glad you invented him, Tom."

Her brother suddenly flushed as he noticed the grinning, gaping crowd that had collected around them. "Let's get out of here," he muttered, "before we get arrested for blocking the sidewalk!"

He and the girls hurried off to the parking lot. Fido rolled along behind them, amid gawking exclamations from passers-by. The radio guidance mechanism kept him lined up a few feet in back of Elsa all the way. At the parking lot Tom lifted the robot dog into the back seat of Phyl's white convertible.

Sandy asked, "What'll Elsa do if she wants to go for a ride when you're not around? I mean, who'll lift him into the car?"

"Nothing to it," Tom said. "His body's made of lightweight plastic and his electronic gear is all microminiaturized. Fido's a tough-looking brute, but he's not heavy."

The white convertible pulled out of the lot and Tom waved good-by. Bud was waiting for him in the panel truck. As the two boys drove back to Swift Enterprises, Bud chuckled.

"Quite a little monster you created there, genius boy. Elsa's going to be the most stared-at girl in Shopton!"

"That's partly what I had in mind when I dreamed him up," Tom confided. "I doubt that our unknown enemy will dare try anything against Elsa while she's a focus of public attention."

Bud grinned as he turned onto the highway that ran out of town and past the experimental plant. "If you really want to nail your enemy," he suggested, "you ought to make Fido a blood-hound who could even follow a crook's trail."

"That's a swell idea," Tom said.

At once his alert brain began toying with the possibility. "You know, Bud, that *could* be done," he remarked thoughtfully, "just by adapting the principle of the aquatomic tracker to air scents instead of chemical traces in water."

Tom was referring to a device he had invented and installed on his diving seacopter for tracking ships or other objects at sea.

"Forget I said it," Bud joked. "Don't you ever give that brain of yours a rest, pal? Maybe a little music would help."

Bud flipped on the dashboard radio and switched to some catchy Calypso music. As the piece ended, the disk jockey said:

"Hold it, fans—they've just handed me a news bulletin. Another outburst of shrill, blasting sounds, like those recently heard in Detroit, has just cut loose in San Francisco! The sounds began only minutes ago, at 10:17 A.M. Pacific Daylight Time, but traffic is already badly snarled and the city is in an uproar. The source of the sounds is a total mystery."

Tom threw Bud a startled glance. "Step on it,

fly-boy! I want to contact Ted Elheimer and get a firsthand report on this!" Elheimer was the West Coast telecaster of the Swifts' private television network.

The boys were already approaching the walls of the vast experimental station. Bud speeded up, and moments later, their panel truck was rolling through the gate. As it halted near the Main Building, the two youths leaped out and ran inside.

As they rushed into the Swifts' spacious modernistic double office, Tom's father looked up in surprise from his work-littered desk.

"Anything wrong, son?"

"Plenty, Dad! Frisco's being hit by those same sounds we heard in Detroit!"

Tom dashed toward a giant control panel set into one wall of the office. A red light was already flashing, signaling an incoming call. He flicked on the videophone. Ted Elheimer's face settled into focus on the screen and a torrent of shrill noise came blasting out of the speaker. Tom hastily toned it down.

"We're having a sonic blitz here," the telecaster reported, shouting to make himself heard. "I thought you would be interested."

"We sure are, Ted!" Tom replied. "What's the latest?"

"Just what you see here—and it's getting worse

by the minute!" Elheimer, who was broadcasting outdoors, stepped aside to let the camera pan over the street. It revealed a wild tangle of traffic and panic-stricken pedestrians rushing to and fro, clutching their ears. "I have two mobile camera crews roving the city," he went on. "Stand by and I'll cut 'em in."

Other scenes of chaos followed. As in Detroit, the shrieking sounds were undulating up and down in pitch weirdly. Even as they came over the speaker, the effect was terrifying. Tom could feel his own pulse racing.

"Any clue to the source yet?" Mr. Swift inquired.

"Not a hint so far," Elheimer replied. "The police and Civil Defense authorities are trying to localize the sounds, but the people I've checked with admit they're baffled. That sort of thing takes time and instrumentation and they're just not set up for it."

Bud, meanwhile, had switched on a transistor radio and was getting a network broadcast from the scene. Traffic accidents and ambulance calls were being reported at an alarming rate.

"The wildest sort of speculation is going on about the cause," a newscaster said. "A university professor, who asked that his name be withheld, has raised the possibility that the sounds are somehow being generated by creatures or signals from outer space. And Swami Fazir, leader of a local

religious sect, has just phoned in an announcement that the end of the world may be at hand!"

"Wow! Did you hear that?" Bud said.

"The sounds are diminishing, I think!" Ted
Elheimer reported suddenly.

Within seconds, they faded completely. Just
then the telephone rang in the office. Tom answered.

The caller was Dan Perkins, editor of the *Shopton Bulletin*. "Tom," he said, "can you and your
father offer any theory to explain those crazy
sounds out in San Francisco?"

"Sorry, Dan. We honestly can't," the young inventor replied. "If you can dig up a reasonable
explanation, we'd like to hear it."

After hanging up, Tom stood in deep thought
for a moment. "Dad," he said, "do you suppose
our space friends know anything about this?"

"It's a long shot but worth finding out, son.
Why not give them a call?"

Some time before, a strange black missile had
plunged to earth on the grounds of Swift Enterprises. It was covered with symbols which proved
to be a message in mathematical code from creatures on another planet. The Swifts had cracked
the code and succeeded in establishing radio com-
munication with the unknown beings.

Tom and Bud jeeped at once to the space communications lab. Here, Tom pounded out a message on the keyboard of the electronic brain which

automatically coded and decoded the space mes-
sages. Soon a signal bell announced an answer and
the reply was typed out on tape:

> WE KNOW NOTHING OF ANY SUCH PHE-
> NOMENON BUT WILL INVESTIGATE.

By evening the Swifts had heard nothing more.
Disappointed, the family and Elsa sat down to
dinner. Presently the doorbell rang insistently.
Tom left the table and found Harlan Ames standing on the front porch. He was excited.

"Tom," he exclaimed, "I've just had a strange
report on John Wyvern! It came from Australia!"

CHAPTER VII

DOWN UNDER

"COME on in, Harlan!" Tom stepped aside from the doorway to let the security man enter, then lowered his voice. "Is the news good or bad?"

"Could be either—it's hard to tell."

Tom paused for a moment, then said, "We may as well let Elsa hear it directly."

He led the way into the dining room. A place was made at the table for Ames, and Mrs. Swift poured him a cup of coffee. Elsa Wyvern was wide-eyed as she hung eagerly on his words.

"The FBI had Interpol—the International Police Organization—circulate your father's description all over the world," Ames told her. "Now they've had a cablegram from Sydney, Australia. It says a police sergeant at Alice Springs reported that a rancher's plane had sighted three words scrawled in the sand—apparently so they could be seen from the air. The words were: '*John Wyvern—Help*'!"

Elsa gasped. "Is Alice Springs in some remote part of Australia?"

"It's in the Northern Territory," Ames replied, "which is big and empty and mostly unsettled— part of what the Aussies call the Outback. The police assume that whoever made the sign must be lost and wandering somewhere on the wasteland. An air search is under way, but so far no results have been reported."

"Oh, Elsa! I'm so glad there's a clue at last!" Sandy burst out sympathetically. "Somehow I feel sure your dad's still alive!"

"Thanks, Sandy—I feel the same way." Elsa's eyes filled with tears of hope. "But goodness, how did he ever get so far away as Australia? I wonder if I should go there . . ."

Tom turned to his father. "Dad, I think we have a stake in this—maybe a big stake, in view of those two bombing attempts. How about Bud and me hopping down there in the Flying Lab and taking Elsa?"

"Good idea, son," Mr. Swift agreed. "You may be able to help in the search."

Sandy, her blue eyes sparkling with excitement, demanded, "What about me?"

Her brother grinned. "Okay. You and Phyl both. We'll leave on Sunday if there's no further word from the Australian authorities."

Arrangements were hastily made. Tom telephoned Bud, and Sandy called the Newtons. Phyl, regretfully, was unable to go since she was about to take a vacation trip with her mother.

As Tom was getting ready for bed that night he recalled Bud's remark about Elsa's watchdog. "Maybe I should follow up on that—just in case," the younger inventor mused.

Saturday morning at the plant Tom broke off work on his Silentenna Mark II long enough to make several sketches and diagrams. He turned these over to Arv Hanson.

"Rush this into production for me on Monday, will you?" Tom asked.

The big technician nodded genially as he pored over the plans. "Sure thing, skipper. But why wait? I'll start work on it today."

At noon Chow Winkler wheeled a lunch cart into Tom's lab. The roly-poly Texan had an aggrieved look on his leathery face. "You ain't aimin' to take off on this trip down under without a cook, are you, Tom?"

"Shucks no, pardner. Want to come along?"

"I'm rarin' to go, boss!" Chow brightened at once and went back to his galley, whistling a loud, perky cowboy ballad.

Early on Sunday Tom made an overseas telephone call to Australia. The police there had no fresh word on John Wyvern. That afternoon Tom's party took off in the *Sky Queen*. Besides

Tom, Bud, Sandy, Elsa, and Chow, three Swift crewmen were abroad. One was Hank Sterling, Enterprises' quiet but two-fisted chief engineer and troubleshooter.

Cruising at Mach 3, the Flying Lab streaked down out of the skies over the great Pacific island continent about five hours later. Passing above the Great Barrier Reef and the settled eastern State of Queensland with its snow-capped Great Dividing Range, they headed westward into the interior.

Soon the country became flatter and more barren. Below them spread a harsh, vivid landscape of reddish-brown desert, rippled by long dunes and ridges, with occasional patches of gray-green scrub. Here and there stood the homestead of a remote ranch.

"Looks sort o' like our own Southwest, don't it?" remarked Chow.

"Yes, and it's great cattle country," Tom told the cook. "The people call their ranches 'cattle stations.' I've read that many of them are as big as two thousand square miles."

Bud chuckled. "Makes those Texas spreads sound pretty dinky, eh, Chow?"

Presently the *Queen* arrowed down toward the neatly laid-out town of Alice Springs, nestled in a spur of purplish-red mountains.

"What time is it here?" Sandy asked.

Tom did some rapid figuring. "Almost ten o'clock Monday morning. Remember, we've passed over the international date line." Seeing Sandy's and Elsa's surprised expressions, he added, "It's midwinter down under, too, but I guess we won't notice it in this part of Australia."

Soon after the huge ship landed, a police car came speeding out on the field to meet them. A tall, brawny, suntanned man in a khaki uniform and broad-brimmed felt hat jumped out of the car. His face split in a friendly grin.

"Welcome to the Red Heart of Australia, cobbers! I'm Sergeant Kincaid of the Territorial Police."

"Cobbers," Tom knew, was Aussie slang for "friends."

He introduced himself and the others. Kincaid said he had been told of their expected arrival by the authorities in Sydney, and he had asked the airfield tower to alert him as soon as their plane approached.

The sergeant drove Tom, Bud, and the girls to the police station in town. The Americans were amazed at the smart shops, blossoming gardens, and modern suburban bungalows in such a remote desert outpost. Many of the streets were lined with cedars, pepper trees, and oleanders.

"What a beautiful place!" Sandy exclaimed.

"Real bonza," Kincaid agreed proudly. "Some say it's the loveliest spot in Australia. People come here to visit and end by settling down for life!"

Tourists mingled with dark-skinned stockmen

in cowboy hats and tight jeans. A screeching flock
of sulphur-crested cockatoos burst from a grove of
orange trees as they drove past.

At the station Sergeant Kincaid briefed the visitors. "An abo on walkabout sighted a white man
near the area where the 'Help' sign was seen," he
began.

"Hold it, sir," put in Bud. "What's an abo on
walkabout?"

"An abo, or aborigine, is a blackfellow—one of
the race that lived in Australia before the white
men came," Kincaid said. "They make fine stockmen, or cowboys. About once a year many of them
get restless, doff their clothes, and head out into
the bush with just a boomerang and a spear. They
call it 'going walkabout.'

"Anyhow," the policeman went on, "this abo
sighted a white man who could be John Wyvern.
But he acted so wild and crazed that the abo was
afraid to go closer."

"Where did this happen?" Tom asked.

"About two hundred fifty miles north of here,
near the Murchison Range, east of the bitumen."
The bitumen, Kincaid added, was the popular
name for the Stuart Highway which ran a thousand miles northward through the Territory from
"the Alice" to Darwin on the coast.

"Hasn't your air search sighted this white man
yet?" Elsa inquired anxiously.

Kincaid shook his head. "No, miss. We think he must move about only at night. But a police tracker has been sent out to pick up his trail, and I guarantee you he'll find your father if anyone can —assuming the man *is* your father."

Tom asked if they might accompany the tracker.

"Sure thing. I planned on joining him as soon as you got here. It'll be a slow business, though, and a plane won't be much use. We'll have to move at the tracker's pace."

Since the search might take days, it was decided that only Tom, Bud, Chow, and the sergeant would take part. Five police horses—one a pack animal laden with supplies—were driven to the field and herded into the *Queen's* hold.

Kincaid sat in the pilot's compartment as they skimmed north above the highway. After a while he pointed below to a cluster of enormous boulders on either side of the bitumen.

"They call those the Devil's Marbles. No one knows how they got there. The abos believed they were eggs laid by a monster snake back in 'the dreaming'—the old days long ago."

Kincaid told Tom to veer eastward. Presently Bud cried out, "Look! There's the sign!"

Huge letters had been gouged in the sand. Though drifted over, the words could still be made out: JOHN WYVERN—HELP!

The Flying Lab circled the area at high altitude. Through binoculars, Kincaid spied a lone rider traversing the rust-colored flats.

"There's our tracker," he said.

Tom landed nearby. The man, who wore torn, faded dungarees, rode over to the *Queen* and dismounted to meet the visitors. He was dark-skinned, with a wide nose and curly, grizzled hair.

"This is Ben, our tracker." Kincaid introduced the others.

"Good day-ee!" said Ben.

They noticed that the blackfellow, though spindly legged, seemed to be wiry and strong, and stood very erect. Chow eyed his spurred boots. Unlike Texas-style boots, they had elastic sides and thin soles.

Kincaid asked about the trail. Ben said the white man seemed to be traveling in a circle.

"Think he's wonky?" the sergeant asked.

"Too right. Probably crook from the sun."

Kincaid explained that this meant the man was out of his mind and probably ill.

"How can Ben tell?" Bud asked in surprise.

The sergeant chuckled. "Not much gets by you abo trackers, eh, Ben? When they trail a man, they can almost tell what he's thinking!"

The group unloaded the horses, then had lunch.

Tom told Hank Sterling to scout the area from

"Look!" Bud cried. "There's the sign!"

the air. "Unless you sight Wyvern, fly the *Queen* back to Alice Springs and stand by."

The search party started out on horseback. Hour after hour the animals plodded across the dusty, brass-sunned wasteland. From time to time Ben dismounted to study the ground for tracks which were too faint for even Chow to distinguish.

Shadows gathered late in the afternoon. Ben drew rein and pointed behind them. Two weird reddish columns were moving swiftly toward the riders.

"Good grief! What are those?" Bud gasped.

"Willi-willies," said Sergeant Kincaid. "A kind of dust storm we get here on the Outback."

The whirling pillars passed close by with a roar and a stinging spray of sand.

"Wow! I'm glad that missed us!" cried Bud.

At sundown the party made camp and Ben built a fire of brushwood. Chow quickly cooked a tasty supper. Then they spread their "swags," or blanket rolls, and were soon fast asleep.

Tom awoke with a start under a night sky sprinkled with stars. A din of stampeding hoofs was thundering toward them out of the darkness! Someone yanked his arm.

"Look out, mates!" yelled Sergeant Kincaid. "It's a flamin' mob of wild brumbies!"

CHAPTER VIII

MADMAN'S TRAIL

BRUMBIES? For a moment Tom was confused. Then, as his eyes adjusted to the moonlit darkness, he could make out the plunging forms and flying manes of horses in an onrushing herd.

Bud and Chow were scrambling out of their blankets. "Wh-what's going on?" Bud stammered.

"A wild-horse stampede!" Tom exclaimed.

Their own mounts, tethered to rocks, were snorting and whinnying in fright. The boys and Chow struggled to calm them.

Ben had snatched a stick from the pile of brushwood and lit it in the glowing campfire. He waved the blazing brand. Meanwhile, Kincaid levered shells into his rifle and fired a series of shots into the air.

Frightened, the wild horses veered away and went clattering off.

Kincaid lowered his rifle. "Never seen bush horses cut up like that at night before."

"Mebbe somethin' spooked 'em," put in Chow.

Ben nodded. "Them come from over that ridge yonder. Could be some chap stirred 'em up—oh—!"

He paused as the eerie howl of a wild dog split the air.

"Dingoes," said the sergeant. "That's probably the answer."

There were no more disturbances and at dawn the group broke camp and resumed the trail. The sandy waste was dotted with tufts of bristling spinifex grass, saltbush, and mulga scrub. Among them rose queer-looking knee-high mounds.

"Anthills," explained Kincaid. "Up near the tropics they rise eight feet tall."

To the north the horizon was broken by the low-lying scarps and ridges of the Murchison Range. Apparently the man they were following was making his way in that direction. But all they saw were a grazing herd of kangaroos and an ostrich-like emu that scampered off at their approach.

In midmorning Ben made out fresh "signs" in the sandy soil. "Blackfellers," he announced.

"Uncivilized natives?" Tom asked.

Kincaid nodded. "Half-wild blacks from the government reserve in the Davenport Hills."

"Probably Chief Nabbari's mob," Ben added.

An hour later the searchers sighted a grove of eucalyptus along the banks of a creek. Feathery smoke drifted upward.

"That's where the abos are camped," said the sergeant. "Must be having a corroboree."

"What's that?" said Bud.

"Sort of a song-and-dance feast."

The medicinal scent of eucalyptus from the white-trunked ghost gum trees greeted their nostrils as they approached. It mingled with the scent of cooking meat. The three Americans were startled by the jackass laugh of a kookaburra bird, perched in the tree branches.

About forty natives squatted around the campfire. They arose as the travelers came closer and dismounted. The lubras, or women, in ragged dresses, clutched their babies across their hips and retired into the brush-and-earth "humpies" which had been built near the creek.

The men were half-naked, with their heads circled by snakeskin bands. Dilly bags, for their tobacco and personal possessions, hung around their necks. The adults were bearded and had tribal scars on their shoulders and chests. A gray-haired elder faced the policeman.

Kincaid said, "Day-ee, Nabbari. You know why we come here?"

As the chief shrugged, the sergeant went on, "We are looking for lost white fellow. You have seen him?"

Nabbari exchanged darting, uneasy looks with his comrades. "No see."

"He has been close to your camp."

Nabbari avoided the sergeant's accusing gaze. Kincaid took some plugs of tobacco from his pocket and handed them out. Then he got a sack of flour and a sack of sugar from the pack horse. The aborigines eyed them hopefully.

"Now you tell about lost white fellow, eh?"

Nabbari seemed to be getting more and more nervous. "We no see white feller!"

Kincaid's eyes hardened. "Then no tucker for Nabbari," he snapped, and put away the sacks.

As they rode off, the sergeant remarked angrily, "They've seen him, all right—or at least they know he's around—but they aren't talking."

"Too right," said Ben. "They read his tracks easy."

"Then why wouldn't they help us?" Bud asked.

Sergeant Kincaid shook his head. "It's hard to figure these bushmen. If Wyvern's out of his mind, they may be frightened of him. They're superstitious about such things."

Tom wondered if the blackfellows' fear might be due to some more sinister reason.

"What was that grub they were eatin'?" put in Chow.

"Mostly kangaroo," said Kincaid, "along with some bugs, worms, rodents—things like that."

The roly-poly Texan shuddered. "I'm sure glad they didn't invite us to stay to lunch."

As the day wore on, Ben paused more and more often to study the ground. He reported that the tracks were fresh and their quarry not far ahead.

The sky flamed red and gold as twilight closed in over the Outback. They made camp among the rocky outcrops of the Murchison Range. As they ate, Ben cast frequent glances all around.

"Something wrong?" inquired Kincaid.

The tracker shrugged uneasily. "Don't know, boss. Got a feeling we're being watched."

As they finished the meal, Ben looked up sharply. "I heard something!" he muttered.

The tracker darted away from the fire into the gathering darkness. Dimly the others could make out Ben's figure clambering up the rugged slope that overlooked their camp.

A few moments later the stillness was shattered by a scream of pain! Then came the thud of a falling body.

"That's Ben!" exclaimed Kincaid. He snatched a torch from the fire and started toward the sound. The others followed.

Ben was soon found, lying head downward on the slope—his shoulder pierced by a long, stone-tipped spear. Awkwardly but gently, they carried him back to the campfire.

The tracker was unconscious. Kincaid was pale with rage over the cowardly attack, but he knew it was hopeless to find the assailant in the darkness. He removed the spear and dressed Ben's wound as best he could.

"That looks bad," Tom muttered. "The

wound's close to his chest. He'd better not be moved."

"We can call the Royal Flying Doctor Service," said Kincaid.

Tom did so over the two-way radio he had brought and also summoned the *Sky Queen*. Kincaid brooded gloomily as they waited.

"It may not be easy to find another tracker to replace Ben," he said. "You saw how the abos acted when we asked about Wyvern."

"Leave that to me," said Tom.

The *Queen* reached their campsite first, followed later by the R.F.D.S. plane. A young Australian doctor gave Ben emergency treatment and said that he must be flown to a hospital.

"I know your plane's fitted for ambulance service," said Tom, "but ours is faster and may be more comfortable for the patient. Would you care to use it?"

The doctor gladly accepted. But Kincaid vowed, "I'm not leaving here until I find the bloke who speared Ben."

"I'll stick with you, pardner," said Chow.

En route to Alice Springs, Tom radioed Enterprises, knowing that it would be early morning in Shopton. He asked for Arv Hanson.

"How about that gear I sketched out Saturday, Arv?" Tom inquired. "Is it almost ready?"

"Finished it last night, skipper. I was going to check it out this morning."

"Great. As soon as it's all set, hop down here on a cargo jet," Tom ordered. "And catch some shut-eye on the way. One thing more—bring that suitcase of Wyvern's clothes."

Ben was rushed to the Alice Springs Hospital. Later the doctor reported that he would recover. But the tracker could provide no clue to the mysterious spearman.

Tom and Bud bunked aboard the Flying Lab that night. Next morning the young inventor checked by radio with Chow and Sergeant Kincaid.

"I've been over to the abos' camp," said Kincaid. "Nabbari swears none of his men did the spearing and I think he's telling the truth." Tom advised the sergeant to stand by.

The two boys had lunch with Sandy and Elsa. Sandy told of their visit to Ayers Rock, a huge red monolith full of ancient cave paintings.

Tom mystified both girls by saying to Elsa, "I'd like to borrow your faithful pooch. He's about to turn into a real bloodhound."

Arv's cargo jet arrived at one o'clock, after a ten-hour flight. Doc Simpson, Swift Enterprises' young physician, had also come along in case Wyvern needed medical attention.

Everyone watched with keen interest as Tom installed the newly arrived gear in Fido. Five vacuum hoses now projected out in front of the mobile robot.

"They'll draw up scent traces just as a bloodhound does through his nostrils," Tom explained. "A repello-spectrograph analyzer will compare these with a sample scent fed in at the start. And Fido's guidance mechanism will keep the center hose always lined up on the trail."

Bud chuckled. "This I have to see!"

The *Queen* flew the boys, Arv, and Doc north over the Outback and dropped them at the camp. Kincaid whistled and scratched his head as Tom explained how he hoped to use Fido.

Using a much-worn sweater of Wyvern's, Tom tuned the repello-spectrograph to detect the proper scent molecules. Then, with a radio control, he started Fido off.

The automaton rumbled over the broken, rocky ground for several hours. Dusk fell, but after a halt for supper, Tom insisted upon continuing. He pressed a switch and the crystal lenses on Fido's collar shone with a brilliant light that illuminated the ground in all directions.

The trail led over a low ridge, then through a pass into open terrain carpeted with spinifex grass and scrub. But Fido veered toward a dark opening among the rocks on their left.

"It's a cave!" Bud exclaimed.

Suddenly an eerie scream sounded from within!

CHAPTER IX

DIDJERIDOO

THE searchers froze in their saddles. In spite of Tom's steady nerves, a chill of fear prickled his neck at the unearthly shriek from the cave.

"Good grief!" Arv whispered hoarsely. "Was that *human?*"

"I'd say half-human," muttered Sergeant Kincaid. "If our man's in there, blimey, he must be in a bad way!"

Tom gripped a small portable repelatron that he had brought from the *Sky Queen,* in case of further danger. This device beamed out a repelling force which he had made use of in his deepsea hydrodome, and later in his great moon ship, the *Challenger.*

"Better let me go first," Tom said.

Dismounting, they advanced toward the opening. Fido had halted at the cave mouth on a radio signal from Tom's control box. The white brilliance of his collar lights probed the darkness within, but no sign of life could be seen.

Tom made his way past the robot, keeping his repelatron ready. Inside, the opening widened into a deep, shadowy cavern.

A sudden whimpering sound made Tom's scalp bristle! He whirled and saw the figure of a man trying to flatten himself out of sight against the rock wall to Tom's left.

John Wyvern!

The scientist was a pitiable sight—gaunt as a skeleton, his shirt and trousers in filthy tatters. His face, brick red from the sun, was fringed with a sandy growth of beard. He seemed wild-eyed with fear.

"Roarin' rockets! Don't tell me that's Wyvern!" Bud gasped. He and the others were crowding into the cave behind Tom.

"Stay away! D-d-don't touch me!" Wyvern screeched. He began to gibber insanely.

"Easy there, mate," Kincaid said soothingly.

Wyvern's right hand was clenched into a tight fist—apparently clutching something. But the broken-nailed fingers of his other hand were like claws. He seemed ready to resist ferociously if they moved a step nearer.

"Hold it!" Tom warned his companions. He braced the repelatron against a spur of rock and flicked it on.

Seeing Tom aim the device, Wyvern tried to hurl himself at the young inventor. But the force of the repulsion beam pinned him back against the rock wall! The crazed fugitive writhed and struggled, his red-rimmed eyes bulging, but he was powerless against the invisible barrier of the repelatron beam.

"We're your friends, Dr. Wyvern!" Tom said urgently. "We've come to rescue you!"

Once convinced that the group intended no harm, Wyvern's belligerence subsided. The brawny sergeant, assisted by Bud and Arv, led him away from the cave wall and into the light, where Doc Simpson could examine him.

Tom gently pried open Wyvern's fist. Inside was a rough but beautiful blue-black stone flecked with red, gold, and green.

"Wow! What kind of stone is that?" Bud asked.

Tom held up the gem. Its colors shimmered in the light. "Unless I'm mistaken, it's a raw opal."

"You've guessed it, cobber," said Sergeant Kincaid. "That's a black opal—worth a tidy packet, too, I'd say! Cor, I wonder where he picked that up."

Meanwhile, Doc was examining the haggard scientist. Wyvern replied to the medic's questions in incoherent mumbles.

"Think he's been doped?" Tom asked.

"No—not recently, anyhow." Doc seemed to be

puzzled. "He may be out of his mind just from hardship and exhaustion. . . . Or, it *could* be due to some sort of brainwashing."

"Brainwashing?" Tom stared at the young medic. "Exactly what kind?"

Doc shrugged, frowning. "I hardly know myself, skipper. But suppose he was kidnapped. His captors may have mistreated him or subjected him to some kind of psychological torture that brought on a mental breakdown."

"Hmm, I see. Going to give him a sedative?"

"Not as long as he stays quiet," said Doc. "I may as well keep him on his feet until we can get him into a hospital bed."

"Okay. I'll call the *Sky Queen* right now."

Tom tuned up their transceiver and radioed the Flying Lab at Alice Springs. After breaking the good news that Wyvern had been found alive, he asked Hank Sterling to come and pick them up.

Hank, however, reported that their landing gear had been damaged when he set down at the airfield. "We're still working on it, Tom. Be at least an hour before we can take off."

"Understood," Tom replied. "But make it as quickly as possible, Hank."

They settled in the cave to wait. Outside, Chow made a fire, put on a "billy" can of tea, and cooked a meal for the patient. Wyvern ate greedily.

"It's a wonder the poor guy didn't starve—or die of thirst," Arv remarked.

"The abos may have set out tucker for him, or he may have been lucky enough to bring down some lizards or small game with a stone," Kincaid said. "The billabong—the creek—where the blacks were camped would provide water. So would certain plants."

"What I'd like to know is where he got that stone," said Tom. "Any ideas, Sergeant?"

"Well, a number of people in the Territory have loose opals they get in one place or another.

There's a whole collection on display back at Alice. Far as I know, though, no precious opal like this is found right *in* the Territory, although some common stuff has been picked up on the South Alligator River."

As he sipped his "cuppa," Kincaid studied the stone in the light. "The nearest real diggings are down at Coober Pedy and Andamooka in South Australia. But black opals come mostly from Lightning Ridge over in New South Wales."

"Could he have picked this up, right off the ground?" Bud asked.

The sergeant nodded. "Yes, some mighty rich lodes have been stumbled on just that way."

"Do you suppose Wyvern knew all along about some opal lode down here?" Arv put in.

"And he came to Australia for that reason, you mean?" said Tom.

"Sure. Maybe he had partners who made a secret opal strike. Wyvern came down to claim his share, but they double-crossed him and dumped him here on the Outback to die."

Tom rubbed his jaw thoughtfully. "It's an interesting theory, Arv, but how about this? Wyvern came to Detroit all set to read a scientific paper. I can't imagine him ducking out from that and leaving Elsa without a word."

"It wouldn't explain who speared our tracker, either," Bud argued. "Unless Wyvern did it himself. Think he could have, Sarge?"

"Reckon it's possible," said Kincaid. "But I doubt it. These native spears aren't easy to toss. The one that got Ben must have been hurled with pretty good force—probably with a woomera, or spear thrower, as the abos do it."

To pass the time, Tom tuned the radio to a musical program being broadcast from a Darwin station. It was approaching nine-thirty, or a half hour later on Australia's east coast. Presently the Australian Broadcasting Commission's ten o'clock news from Sydney came on.

Tom and his companions were startled as the announcer said:

"Another city in the U.S.A. has just been assailed by the same weird sounds heard in Detroit and San Francisco! This time, the outburst occurred in Atlanta, Georgia. The shrill noises broke loose in full fury as the morning rush hour was getting under way. Highways into the city were turned to bedlam. Numerous traffic accidents occurred and more than fifty people were hospitalized from various causes before the sounds ceased half an hour later."

"Jumpin' jets! It's happened again!" Bud gasped.

"But the excitement was not over," the announcer went on. "Soon after, the major American news agencies received anonymous phone tips that a warning was being sent to the United States Government. The warning stated that what happened to the three cities already blitzed was just a sample of worse to come.

"Unless the government agreed to certain terms, a *prolonged* sonic attack would be unleashed against still another city—throwing it into utter chaos and endangering thousands of lives! The terms were not told. As yet, there is no word from Washington on any such message."

"Great sizzlin' steaks!" Chow blurted out. "What in tarnation's goin' on back home?"

"It could be deadly serious if the threat is carried out," Tom said worriedly. "Fifty people in Atlanta were hospitalized after half an hour, but there's no telling how many more were near breakdown. From what Dr. Kimer told me about sound stress, there might be hundreds—even thousands —dead or dying if a city had to take those sounds much longer."

His listeners were appalled. Chow asked, "What sort of sidewinders would do such a thing?"

Before Tom could reply, an eerie, booming sound broke the darkness. Its low, vibrating tone wavered up and down in a strange rhythm.

"What in blazes is that?" Arv exclaimed.

"A didjeridoo!" said Kincaid. "It's a long wooden tube the abos blow to summon spirits."

The Americans looked at one another uneasily.

"They may be nearby, watching us," Bud muttered. "Maybe the same ones who speared Ben!"

"This time *I'll* go look," said Kincaid.

"Not alone!" Tom gripped his repelatron.

It was decided that Tom, Bud, and Chow would accompany the sergeant. The weird booming notes continued as the group left the cave. Tom carried his flashlight; the others blazing torches.

The sounds appeared to be coming from somewhere in the pass. But it veered off across the slopes and rocky upthrusts. After a time it faded into silence. Baffled, Tom and his companions returned to camp.

As they approached the cave, all of them stopped short in horror. Two figures lay sprawled unconscious on the ground.

"Arv and Doc!" Bud cried out.

CHAPTER X

FIERY OMENS

THE two men lay face down and motionless in the flickering light from the campfire. Tom, fearing the worst, rushed toward them.

"Arv! . . . Doc!" the young inventor exclaimed. He rolled Arv over gently but could see no sign of a wound.

"They've been bashed on the head," Sergeant Kincaid muttered, fingering a lump just above the hairline on the back of Doc Simpson's skull. "This one's still breathing, though."

Arv Hanson was, too, Tom realized with relief. But the horses had been driven off.

Bud, meanwhile, had gone into the cave. He emerged, grim-faced. "Wyvern's gone!" he reported.

Tom looked up in dismay.

"That's not all," Bud went on. "Come and take a look at Fido!"

Tom sprang to his feet and strode past the campfire into the cave. He saw at a glance that the robot had been wrecked. Both its head and plastic body had been cracked open, apparently by heavy blows, and the electronic circuitry inside hastily ripped apart.

"Oh, *no!*" Tom gave a groan of despair.

Fighting down bitter anger, Tom hurried out of the cave to help Sergeant Kincaid revive the two victims. Chow was down on his hands and knees, scrutinizing the ground.

"One hombre who came here probably was a blackfellow, boss," the Texan reported. "See here? You kin jest barely make out a naked footprint."

"Must've been more than one," Bud put in.

"Yep, I'd say so, but mebbe not all barefoot. Ground's too hard an' scuffed up to tell much. Looks like there was a struggle."

Chow got to his feet and walked forward to peer at the brush near the edge of the firelight. "Then they made off in that direction."

"Almost due north," Tom noted, after glancing at the position of the four stars forming the Southern Cross. "They must be heading away from the Murchisons into open country."

"They sure didn't go through the pass," Bud agreed, "or we'd have seen them."

By now Doc and Arv were showing signs of coming around. As soon as they had recovered consciousness and felt fit enough to talk, they told their story.

"After you guys left, a blackfellow came up to the campfire," Arv reported. "He acted friendly enough—and very excited. We couldn't understand his jabber, but he kept making signs as if he wanted to show us something."

"And like a couple of chumps we fell for it," Doc added, wincing. "He must have had pals. As we came out of the cave, something hit me from behind."

"We *both* got conked," Arv said ruefully.

The two men were shocked and shamefaced when they learned that Wyvern was gone.

"We sure weren't using our heads—except for targets," Doc Simpson said gloomily.

"Forget it. Any of us might have reacted the same way," said Tom. "The worst of it is, with Fido wrecked, there's no way to trail them." The inventor was gloomy. "I don't suppose you got a look at the guys who hit you—I mean, to know if they were aborigines?"

Doc shook his head. "Not a peek."

"Neither did I," said Arv.

"Look," Bud said, "how do we know Wyvern didn't go along with them willingly? The raiders may have been friends of his, and figured they were rescuing him from *us*."

"I guess the answer is, we don't know," Tom admitted.

Soon afterward, the *Sky Queen's* lights were sighted in the darkness, and the mammoth plane landed near the cave.

Tom dreaded having to tell Elsa of her father's second disappearance. She had been so eager to see him again, alive and safe, that the news came as a cruel shock. Sandy tried to comfort her friend, but Elsa could not hold back tears.

"There's not much we can do tonight," Tom said lamely, "but I promise you I'll have Fido repaired by tomorrow morning. After that, it should be just a question of time before we track your dad down again."

His companions went to bed, weary and worried, in the *Sky Queen's* comfortable sleeping compartments. Tom set to work in the plane's well-equipped laboratory cubicles.

Arv had volunteered to assist him. The model-maker quickly molded a plastic replacement for Fido's shattered head and body. In the meantime, Tom busied himself intently over the automaton's complex tangle of circuitry. As soon as the plastic housing was fabricated, Arv was able to take over some of the reassembly work, using a soldering gun and screwdriver. Tom checked the delicate solid-state and thin-film components.

About two in the morning Arv gave up, heavy-lidded with exhaustion, and flung himself into a bunk. Tom continued for another hour until the repairs were completed. Then he slumped his head on the workbench and fell sound asleep.

Almost at once, it seemed, he was being shaken awake. Tom lifted his head groggily and saw the blond, square-jawed face of Hank Sterling.

"Huh? . . . What's wrong?"

"Take a look out the window, skipper!"

Snapping alert, Tom jumped to his feet and peered out into the darkness. *Balls of fire were rolling along the ground!* Since they were coming from somewhere behind the plane, it was impossible to see the source, but the sky astern was lit by a weird glow.

Tom's face paled. "I think that's what the Aussies call buckbush, Hank—like our tumbleweed! It must be wind-driven from a bush fire!"

The two ran through a passageway from the lab compartment, then down a steel ladder and out the plane's entry hatch.

Tom saw at once that his guess had been right. The entire plain to the north seemed to be blanketed by a sheet of flame! Here and there, an especially reddish patch burst out as a scrub tree caught fire and glowed like a torch.

Tom and Hank were appalled. Already they could feel a searing wave of heat from the blaze. Panic-stricken animals—wallabies, kangaroos, and wild dogs—were scampering through the darkness, heading for the safety of higher ground in the hills of the Murchison Range.

"Good night! It's awful!" Hank muttered.

"Lucky you spotted it this soon. What woke you up?"

"I thought I heard a noise—maybe it was the roaring fire," Hank replied. "I started to doze off again, but I decided to get up to check. Then I saw those rolling balls of fire."

The flames were racing across the dry brushland, coming closer by the moment.

Tom shuddered. "I hate to think of Wyvern out there! Come on, Hank. Let's get airborne!"

The *Sky Queen* quickly soared aloft. Tom flew a wide, sweeping search pattern in a desperate hope of sighting Wyvern and the men with him. As the raging bush blaze drew closer to the line of hills, there was little chance that anyone in the open could be left alive.

Suddenly the intercom buzzed. The ship's radioman informed Tom that his father was calling from Shopton. Tom switched on his set and gave a report of recent happenings.

"That's terrible, son—terrible! Do you think there's any chance of saving Wyvern?"

"Practically none if he was in the path of the fire," Tom confessed grimly.

"Then I guess you'd better come home," Mr. Swift said. "You and I have been asked to attend an urgent conference in Washington."

"What about, Dad?"

"I think it must have to do with the sonic attack threat. Have you heard about that?"

"Yes, we picked up the news over the radio."

"A good many lives may be at stake here," his father said. "Let's see—it's about three-fifteen in the afternoon here and the meeting's set for eight this evening at the Pentagon. Can you possibly make it?"

"Give me a half-hour's leeway and I'll be there," the young inventor promised.

The radioman had notified the Territorial authorities of the fire. Tom flew a final, hopeless sweep of the terrain without sighting any sign of human life. He also checked on the safety of the aborigines camped south of the hills. Then he headed for Alice Springs.

Elsa, grief-stricken but dry-eyed, was determined to stay on and press the search for her father. Sergeant Kincaid recommended a small hotel, owned by a motherly woman, where she might stay. Arv Hanson, too, agreed to remain, and operate Fido in the faint hope of picking up Wyvern's trail when the fire burned out.

After dropping the three at the Alice Springs airfield—along with the *Skeeter,* a midget helicopter which was always carried aboard—the *Sky Queen* zoomed off on its homeward flight across the Pacific. Tom gunned its atomic turbojets and sent the huge craft streaking through the sky at better than Mach 4.

It was exactly three minutes to eight on Wednesday evening when the *Queen* touched down at Dulles International Airport outside Washington, D. C. Mr. Swift had a taxi waiting to rush Tom and himself to the Pentagon, where they made their way inside past a swarm of eager newsmen.

A number of top government scientists and defense officials had already taken their places at the conference table when Tom and his father walked into the meeting room.

Martin Frome, Assistant Secretary of Defense, greeted the two and called the meeting to order. His face was grim as he began, "Gentlemen, America is being threatened by an unknown enemy within our very borders!"

CHAPTER XI

DOOM DIVE

"AN unsigned letter to the President was received in this morning's mail," Frome went on. "I'll read you its contents."

He paused to pick up a typewritten paper.

" 'Sir: You have already seen—in Detroit, San Francisco, and Atlanta—what can happen to a city under sonic attack. Any city, from coast to coast, is just as vulnerable.

" 'But the three attacks so far have been only a sample—mere fleabites. Under a prolonged, all-out sonic blitz, a city could be reduced to utter chaos, with all traffic and communications disrupted, and thousands dead or hospitalized.

" 'We have no wish to carry out such an attack. But the choice is yours, Mr. President. You can prevent it by the payment of ten million dollars —a trifling sum to such a country as the U.S.A.

" 'If you do *not* pay, a major American city will be ruthlessly sound-blitzed. Our demand for payment will then be repeated—this time for *fifty* million dollars—and another city will become a target for attack.

" 'You have ten days in which to issue a public statement agreeing to our terms. You will then receive instructions on how to pay the ten million. If not, the responsibility for what follows will be yours!' "

There was an appalled silence as the Assistant Secretary finished speaking. Then a hard-bitten, gray-haired Army general growled:

"We can't possibly knuckle under to such an outrage! It would make America a laughingstock! We'd be confessing to the world that we were helpless against such an attack!"

"The fact is we *are* helpless," Frome pointed out. "We don't even know where the attack may occur. Unless we're prepared to evacuate every large city before the deadline, the result could be a major disaster."

A Cabinet official toyed uneasily with a pencil. Clearing his throat, he murmured, "Ten million is indeed a small sum, gentlemen, compared to what our government must spend every day for far less urgent matters. Perhaps it would be wisest to pay. Meanwhile, the FBI can be bending every effort to trace the criminals behind this dastardly plot."

"But it's blackmail!" snorted the Army man. "Pay once and we'd pay again and again. No blackmailer's satisfied with a single squeeze!"

"I'm aware of that, General," the official snapped back. "I'm assuming the FBI may be able to nab the criminals before they could strike again. Meantime, we have thousands of lives to consider."

Other voices spoke up. A wrangling debate followed. Several officials stressed the harm to America's prestige and to public respect for law and order, if the blackmail were paid. Another felt sure the method of paying the money would give the FBI a clue to the gang.

Assistant Secretary Frome asked the scientists present for suggestions on how to cope with such an attack. A number of ideas were offered. None seemed likely to be very effective.

Tom whispered a moment with his father. Then he spoke up, "Sir, I'm working on a device that may be able to blank out a sonic attack."

All eyes turned to the young inventor. Tom told of his attempt to design a Silentenna of greater range than his Mark I.

"How near completion is it?" asked Frome.

"The basic concept is all worked out. I believe I can have it ready in forty-eight hours." Tom added that duplicate models could be built and that the *Sky Queen* could fly the device to any city in the country in an hour.

A rush of eager questions followed.

"Tom Swift's opinion is good enough for me!" spoke up Bernt Ahlgren, a top Defense Department research expert.

The Assistant Secretary frowned and stroked his jaw thoughtfully. "Gentlemen, I had better report on this to the White House at once."

Frome excused himself to make a telephone call. Presently he returned.

"The President," Frome said, "has decided to await the results of Tom Swift's project before reaching a final decision. Thank you for your time and advice, gentlemen!"

Reporters were waiting outside, but the Swifts dodged all attempts at an interview. En route to the airport, they saw newspaper extras headlined: SWIFTS SUMMONED TO PENTAGON!

The *Sky Queen* took off. Midway to Shopton, the radioman alerted Tom. "There's a call coming through for you, skipper, but the sender won't identify himself."

Tom flicked on his set. "Tom Swift here."

"Listen good, Swift," a voice snarled over the speaker. "This is the only warning you'll get. Don't proceed with any invention to stop the sonic attack or you'll be our first victim!"

Tom tried to maintain contact, but the voice made no response. Mr. Swift, who was in the compartment, said gravely:

"You've shouldered a big responsibility, Tom.

Now it seems that it may be a dangerous one."

"That threat we heard won't stop me, Dad."

"No, I didn't suppose so. But we'd better have Ames tighten all security measures."

For the next two days Tom worked and slept in his private laboratory at Swift Enterprises. On Saturday a flight test of his Silentenna Mark II was scheduled. Bud, who was to pilot the test, joined Tom for lunch at the lab.

The young flier stared with keen interest at two curious-looking devices suspended horizontally and side by side above Tom's workbench.

Each was about twenty feet long, with a spiral coil of quartz tubing twined around its central axis. From this, three slot-lipped metal fins flared outward along its full length. At either end was a glistening metal ball.

The two devices were connected by cables to an electronic-control console on the workbench.

"So this is your new Silentenna gear," said Bud. "How come you made two?"

"This pair is designed for twin-mounting on the *Sky Queen*—one under each wing," Tom said. "The one you'll test today is a smaller unit to be mounted under your jet's nose."

"Give me the lowdown on how it works."

Tom's eyes twinkled. "You want the full-dress technical explanation or the cut-rate version?"

"Strictly cut-rate, pal—to match my IQ."

"Don't sell yourself short, fly-boy," Tom said

with a grin. "But okay—I'll keep it simple. As you know, sound waves are transmitted through air by to-and-fro vibration of the air molecules."

Bud nodded. "That much I savvy."

"Well, my Mark II damps out their vibration by pulsing out a repelling force at the same frequency. It's as if you were to slow down and stop a playground swing by pushing against it every time it swung toward you."

"Sounds great!" said Bud. "How about that snaky coil of tubing?"

"That's the power tube which generates the pulses," Tom replied. "And those long slots are sample intakes, through which the Silentenna finds out the direction and frequency of the sound waves."

Chow was in the apartment next to the laboratory, setting out lunch for the two boys. "Soup's on, buckaroos!" he called.

As Tom and Bud settled down to eat, Tom explained the procedure for the flight test. "The plane's over in a hangar at the commercial airfield," he said.

"Why not here at Enterprises?"

"There'll be a number of observers and Harlan didn't want them coming inside the plant, now that he has tightened up on security," Tom replied. "The first stage of the test will be to dive the plane to supersonic speed over the airport."

"How come a dive?" Bud asked.

"To better control the point at which you reach Mach 1, so as to make sure we receive the boom at its maximum intensity at the airport." Tom added, "If the Silentenna works okay, then make a series of passes over Shopton—and accelerate as far past Mach 1 as you like."

"I'll swing that baby out to the last mile!" Bud gave a chuckle of anticipation, then reached toward a shelf nearby and switched on a transistor radio. "Hey! I almost forgot! That Yankee-Tigers doubleheader should be on soon!"

Chow was wheeling his empty lunch cart out of the room. "So Buddy boy wants to hear the ball game, does he?" the cook thought slyly. "Reckon now's my chance to get even fer the trick them two played on me a couple weeks ago! I'll blank out their radio with this newfangled Silentenny o' Tom's!"

He halted the cart in the lab and studied the electronic console on Tom's workbench. "Hmm. Wonder how he operates this doodad. Better turn these knobs up all the way."

Chow waited. Nothing seemed to happen.

"Mebbe she's not plugged in," the cook thought. He bent down to peer at the electrical cables extending under the workbench.

Boom! Tom and Bud were startled out of their wits by the loud explosion! In the same instant came an agonized howl from Chow.

"Good grief! What's going on?" Tom gasped.

The boys leaped up and ran into the lab. Chow was clutching the seat of his pants.

"What happened?" Bud asked.

"Some lowdown skunk must 'a' blasted me with a scatter-gun!" Chow bellowed. "I won't be able to sit down fer a week!"

After hearing the whole story, Bud was mystified. But Tom, switching off the equipment, noticed a film of silvery dust specks on the workbench and floor. The young inventor broke into helpless laughter.

"What's so all-fired funny?" Chow demanded.

"I'm afraid you just got peppered with sonic buckshot, pardner!" Tom explained that Chow had turned on, not only the Silentenna, but also a high-powered oscillator used to generate sound waves for testing his invention. "What's more, you had it tuned way up in the ultrasonic range, at almost ten megacycles."

"An' jest what does that mean?" Chow asked.

"The Silentenna doesn't operate at that high a frequency, and your ears couldn't even hear the waves being generated," Tom replied. "But it was just the right frequency to resonate a solid aluminum casting on that bench over there. The casting shattered like they say a wineglass does when a soprano hits high C—in fact, it disintegrated—and you got blasted with aluminum particles."

The boys rushed Chow to the infirmary for first aid. Luckily his injuries were slight.

It was two o'clock when Tom and Bud reached the airport. Government officials and newsmen were on hand to witness the test.

Tom greeted them and introduced Bud. Then he described the flight-test procedure. Presently the plane was wheeled out of the hangar where Hank Sterling and a mechanic had been installing the Silentenna. The craft was a small, twin-engined jet of advanced design, built by the Swift Construction Company.

The officials and newsmen eyed the Silentenna with avid interest. This single-unit model was about eight feet long and suspended under the nose section of the fuselage.

"The mounting will allow the pilot to extend or retract the device," Tom told his audience. "On take-off over a populated area, the Silentenna will be extended as it is now, to serve as a sonic boom trap. Later, after Bud achieves full acceleration and a high enough altitude, he can retract the device close to the fuselage for supersonic cruising. Of course he'd extend it again before descending over another populated area."

Bud climbed aboard and soon the jet was roaring down the runway. Once airborne, he zoomed steeply. As a landmark for the initial point of his dive, Bud had picked a wooded peak near Shopton. By the time it lay directly below him, his altimeter read 30,000 feet.

Bud banked into a 180° turn and lined up on the distant airport. Just beyond it, Lake Carlopa looked like a blue puddle.

"Ready to begin descent!" Bud radioed.

"Understood. Proceed with your dive." Tom and the observers were in the airport tower.

Bud moved the stick forward. The nose dropped and the ship tilted smoothly into its dive. In a moment it was plunging toward its target.

Bud's eyes flicked back and forth, from the terrain below to the Machmeter on his instrument panel. Its needle rose steadily as the jet gathered speed . . . 0.5 . . . 0.7 . . . 0.9.

At 19,500 feet the plane passed Mach 1, sending a train of shock waves down toward the airport. The observers heard a low, muffled explosion roll over the field like a faint peal of thunder.

Tom clenched his fist in disappointment. The Silentenna had failed its first major test! Although the sonic boom was much reduced, his invention was far from completely effective.

Far above, Bud had already hauled back on the stick to pull out of his dive. To his horror, the plane's nose refused to come up!

Bud put all the strength of his husky arms into his effort to overpower the stick. It moved back slightly, but still not enough to recover. The plane was definitely nose-heavy!

To Bud's horror, the plane's nose refused to come up

Instinctively he thumbed the electrical trim-control button to set the floating stabilizer for nose-up. Still no response!

"The trim control must have conked out!" Bud realized.

Beads of sweat began to trickle down his face. Second by second, the ship was plummeting closer to the ground!

Desperately Bud tugged at the manual stand-by. The tabs seemed to be frozen rigid—the plane's nose was like lead!

"Tom!" he screamed into his mike. "It's not recovering! I'm going to crash!"

CHAPTER XII

A STRANGE PROPHECY

BUD'S frantic call struck fear into Tom. The occupants of the tower had already observed that the jet was not pulling out of the dive.

"Have you tried the trim control?" Tom radioed.

"It's not working!"

Aboard the jet, Bud's face was white as he watched the altimeter reading drop backward . . . 11,000 . . . 10,000 . . . 9,000 . . . The ship was plunging like a thunderbolt!

Tom racked his brain in desperation. A bail-out now was almost sure to prove hopeless—not to mention the havoc the jet might wreak on homes or buildings if allowed to crash.

Suddenly Tom seized the microphone. "Bud, jettison the Silentenna!"

"How, skipper?"

"Fire the CO_2 cartridge for emergency lowering of the Silentenna gear in case it jams," Tom ordered. "With the gear already in the extended position, that may pack enough wallop to kick it loose! The slipstream will do the rest!"

Bud obeyed with trembling fingers. The altimeter indicator was passing the 6,000-foot mark. As he fired the cartridge, the Silentenna wrenched loose from its mounting.

An instant later Bud felt a sudden response as the nose lightened! The heavy, eight-foot Silentenna plunged free toward Lake Carlopa!

Bud's heart leaped. The plane was recovering. A massive force of seven G's plastered him to his seat as he eased back on the stick. The pull-out was changing his face to a skull-like mask. He could feel a dizzying "gray-out."

Suddenly the ship was seized by violent vibrations! Bud was pounded to and fro in his seat as if by a thousand trip-hammers.

"I'm approaching an accelerated stall!" he gasped over his mike. "I pulled out too fast!"

His limbs felt heavy as lead. Somehow he managed to inch the stick forward. As if by magic, the vibrations ceased. Then—slowly and cautiously —Bud came back on the stick again.

He was almost brushing the treetops as the jet finally leveled out. Bud sucked in his breath with a gasp of relief, then gunned the throttle and clawed the sky for altitude.

"Nice going, fly-boy!" Tom radioed.

"You take the bow, pal—it would've been curtains for me if you hadn't figured out how to dump the Silentenna!" Bud added gloomily, "This has sure ruined your test."

"Forget that and come in," Tom replied. "My invention didn't really silence the boom."

Bud was still white and shaken when he climbed out of the plane after landing. "The trim definitely malfunctioned," he reported.

"Have Hank check it out," Tom said tersely.

As the plane was rolled into the hangar, he discussed the outcome of the test.

"Your Silentenna, as it now stands, couldn't counter an all-out sonic attack," said a Defense official, "but it may help."

The reporters lingered to hear the results of the plane check-out. The news was grim. Hank said the electrical trim control had been sabotaged in such a fashion that in the dive the floating stabilizer had worked into a nose-down position and the trim could not be recovered.

"You're sure it was sabotage?" Tom asked.

"No doubt about that, skipper." Hank produced a small aneroid device, which, when actuated by a predetermined altitude change, would interrupt the electrical phasing of the trim-control motor. "We removed the inspection plate to the trim motor and found this connected. The plane was flown over here yesterday evening. Someone must have sneaked into the hangar during the night."

Bud glanced at Tom uneasily. "Was any word given out on who would pilot the test? Or that the Silentenna to be used was a duplicate?"

The young inventor shook his head. "No."

"Then the saboteur may have hoped you'd be the pilot, and you *and* your invention would wind up smashed," Bud declared.

The two boys, feeling glum, drove back to the plant. They reported the sabotage to Harlan Ames. Then Tom headed for the Main Building to discuss the situation with his father.

"Don't take it too hard, son. This isn't the first time an invention hasn't proved out," Mr. Swift said, after hearing the full story. "Tell me—do you think the principle of your Mark II is still basically right?"

Tom flung himself into a leather lounge chair. "Yes, I do, Dad. That's partly why the outcome of the test is so hard to take."

"If the principle's right, then it's just a question of finding the bugs," the elder scientist went on. "There's too much at stake to let this throw you. The answer is more work."

After a moment's silence Tom looked up with a rueful grin. "You're right as usual, Dad."

After church on Sunday, the young inventor held several telephone conversations with Pentagon officials at their homes. He was told to carry on urgently with his Silentenna project.

Early Monday morning Tom received a call

from Arv Hanson in Australia. "Any new developments?" Tom asked eagerly.

"Not much," Arv replied. "Sergeant Kincaid and I have completely circled the burnt-out brushland with Fido. We couldn't pick up even the faintest trace of Wyvern."

Tom's heart sank. "Sounds as if he must have perished in the fire then, Arv."

"That's the strange part of it, skipper. We've coptered over the ground a dozen times and can't find any sign of victims."

"But that's impossible!" Tom thought. In a moment he said aloud, "Wait a second, Arv! Hank heard some sort of sound before he spotted the burning buckbush."

"A sound like what?" Arv queried.

"I don't know—but suppose it was the sound of a plane's engines," Tom said.

"A *plane?*"

"Sure. The men who snatched Wyvern from the cave may not have been primitive natives. They may have had a plane standing by on the Outback, or they could have radioed to one."

"I get it!" Arv exclaimed. "You think they set the fire themselves, then took off and maybe circled around a bit to make sure it was spreading in the right direction?"

"Exactly," Tom said. "A fire would prevent us from trailing Wyvern any farther—and also cover any tracks of the plane."

"I'll get Sergeant Kincaid working on that angle," Arv promised. "In the meantime, Elsa and I are going to try another lead."

"Such as?"

"We'll take off for Sydney early tomorrow and see what the gem experts there can tell us about Wyvern's opal."

"Good idea. Let me know what you find out."

Tom did little work the rest of the day except pace the laboratory and pore over circuit diagrams as he groped for some means to improve his Silentenna Mark II.

Late in the afternoon he had a surprise visit from Phyllis Newton. The pretty, dark-haired girl came hurrying excitedly into the lab.

"Phyl!" Tom flushed with pleasure. "When did you get back from your trip?"

"About an hour ago," Phyl said. "I rushed right over to show you *this!*"

She held out a paperback novel of the kind sold on newsstands. Its lurid cover showed panic-stricken people rushing about the streets of a sky-scraper city, clutching their ears or collapsing hysterically.

Tom gaped at the title. *"The Sonic Invaders!* Say, that's really prophetic!"

"Very prophetic," Phyl agreed. "And did you notice who wrote it?"

The author's name was Phineas Gull!

Tom let out a whistle. "When was this published?"

"According to the copyright date, five years ago," Phyl replied. "It belongs to the friends we visited. When I saw it, I realized the author was that queer little man who got so much publicity at the convention."

"He'd probably get a lot more publicity if the newspapers found out he'd written a book with this title. I wonder why he didn't mention it."

"It's probably a silly idea," said Phyl, "but do you suppose that Phineas Gull could have anything to do with those terrible sound attacks? If so, he wouldn't have called attention to his book."

Tom gave a nod. "You could be right."

After Phyl had left, Tom acted on a hunch. He telephoned the paperback publisher and asked to speak to the editor-in-chief. Tom inquired if there were any plans for new printings of the novel.

"I'll tell the world there are!" the editor replied gleefully. "A regular trade publisher is bringing it out in hard cover and investing a fortune in advance publicity! Can you imagine how the public will gobble it up after all the headlines? It'll sell like hot cakes!"

He added that his own company would reap a percentage of the profits, and asked if Tom might be willing to do a special review of the book.

"Thanks, but that's a little out of my line," Tom declined coldly. He hung up, then called Ames and asked him to check on Gull.

The young inventor did not go home until late evening. After a warmed-up supper, he settled into an easy chair and began reading *The Sonic Invaders*. It was well past eleven when he finished. The rest of the family had retired.

"Quite a thriller!" Tom thought.

The story told of an attack on an American city, carried out with powerful sonic waves. Except that the attack was launched by invaders from outer space, the plot was amazingly similar to what had already happened in real life. The story even included an ultimatum to the President of the United States!

Tom scowled. Could the real-life sonic attack threat be a wild, harebrained publicity stunt by Gull to turn his book into a best seller?

"Sounds crazy—but, still and all, that book may earn him a fortune," Tom mused. "And Gull probably has enough technical know-how to cook up some sort of sound generators."

Suddenly there was a tinkle of shattering glass and the room was plunged into darkness. Tom leaped to his feet. A deafening blast of sound struck his eardrums.

With a cry, the young inventor collapsed to the floor!

CHAPTER XIII

CRYSTAL QUEST

UPSTAIRS, the noise had roused the other members of the family. Mr. Swift dashed out of his room to investigate. Mrs. Swift and Sandy followed, pulling on their night-robes.

The living room was in darkness. Mr. Swift pressed a wall switch, then gasped as the light came on. Tom lay crumpled on the floor.

Mrs. Swift gave an anxious cry and they all rushed toward the unconscious youth. Tom's skin was pale and clammy.

"Must be in shock," his father said. "Sandy, get me a blanket, please, to wrap around him."

Although Tom's breathing was quick and shallow, his pulse seemed to be strong enough. Mrs. Swift chafed her son's wrists and passed smelling salts under his nose. In a few moments the young inventor recovered consciousness, and was lifted to a couch.

"We'd better call a doctor," said Mr. Swift, and dialed Doc Simpson.

The medic came right over. He could find no bad aftereffects.

"Tell me what happened," the physician said.

"Something broke that windowpane over there and the bulb of my reading lamp," Tom replied. "Then I heard a terrific blast—it sounded right up close to my ears."

"That must be what caused the shock reaction."

"Right—like those wartime cases Dr. Kimer mentioned, or the two shock victims in Detroit." Tom frowned. "But the glass breakage isn't so easy to explain."

Meanwhile, Mr. Swift and Sandy had gone outside to investigate. The Swifts' home was surrounded by a magnetic field. Anyone entering this field instantly touched off a warning signal inside the house. The Swifts and each of their close friends were equipped with tiny neutralizer devices encased in special wristwatches.

Sandy and her father unkenneled the two bloodhounds, Caesar and Brutus, but found no sign there had been any intruder. Other houses in the neighborhood seemed dark and quiet.

"Apparently no one else in the area was disturbed by the noise," remarked Mr. Swift.

When Tom heard this, he said thoughtfully, "That means the blast of sound must have been beamed at me by some highly directional method that kept the sound waves from spreading—something like the anti-inverse-square-wave principle which I used in my megascope space prober."

"You think that's what broke the window?" Mr. Swift asked.

"No, Dad, the glass was shattered first so the beam could get through. That could have been done by ultrasonic resonance—perhaps by some sort of highly advanced phonon maser. My guess is the whole operation was carried out with equipment in a car that cruised past."

"Another attack by our unknown sonic enemy!" The elder scientist's face was grave.

Next morning Tom reported the attack to Ames. "This is what you call getting close to home!" the security chief remarked. "By the way, I have news of my own. I had dinner with Phineas Gull's literary agent yesterday evening."

"What did you find out?"

"Not much," Ames replied. "According to her, Gull is a queer, elusive sort of guy—likes to surround himself with an aura of mystery. But she did tell me one funny thing about him. A year ago he disappeared for five months."

"Disappeared?" Tom echoed.

"Completely. Even his own agent couldn't get in touch with him. Then he showed up again all of a sudden without a word of explanation."

"Harlan, that could be important!" Tom exclaimed. "It may fit in with that pattern of other disappearances the FBI told you about."

Ames nodded. "That occurred to me, too."

"He may even have been kidnapped and brainwashed into assisting this sonic gang."

"That seems pretty farfetched," Ames objected. "What use would a science-fiction writer be to their scheme?"

Tom shrugged. "You've got me there. But let's not pass up any angles."

"Don't worry. I'm going to pass this information on to Wes Norris of the FBI," Ames said.

Again Tom buried himself in work. He spent hours testing every part and circuit of his Silentenna, seeking ways to make the design more powerful and efficient.

Later in the day, while Tom was staring out a window in the lab, a voice said, "Any progress, son?"

Tom looked around. "Oh—hi, Dad! Didn't hear you come in. No, I'm not making much progress. But I think I've spotted the main flaw."

"In what part of your Silentenna?"

"In the transducer crystals. They just don't respond accurately enough to variations in frequency to match the incoming sounds."

Mr. Swift pondered the problem. "How about using supersmectic liquid crystals?"

"Liquid crystals . . ." Tom gave his father a startled look. "Dad, that's a terrific idea! . . .

"Another attack by our unknown sonic enemy!" said
Mr. Swift

Hmm. But the piezoelectric angle could be pretty tough."

"John Wyvern's been over that ground," Mr. Swift pointed out. "He developed a kind of electromechanical activator that functioned very successfully with liquid crystals."

Tom snapped his fingers enthusiastically. "If I can get one of his activators from the Sonicon labs, it should solve my problem! I'll hop over there right now and see Dr. Kimer about it."

Tom soon took off in one of his triphibian atomicars. These sleek, atomic-powered vehicles could soar over land or water, or convert to sportscar use for highway travel.

In twenty minutes he landed on the parking lot of the Sonicon Research Institute. At the reception desk Tom asked to speak to Dr. Kimer.

The girl on duty recognized the famous young inventor at once. After speaking on the telephone, she said with a smile, "Dr. Kimer is out of his office, but his secretary says to go in and wait. I'll have a guard escort you."

The uniformed plant guard led Tom down a long corridor. They passed a partly opened door that bore the name *Dr. John Wyvern*. Tom stopped with a gasp as he glimpsed a figure inside.

"Hold it a second! Is Dr. Wyvern back?"

"Dr. Wyvern?" The guard turned a startled face to Tom. "No, sir. Why?"

"I thought I saw someone in his lab," the young inventor replied.

Tom pushed the door farther open and stepped into the room. A man stood at an open file cabinet, leafing through papers. He turned.

"Oh . . . Dr. Kimer," said Tom. "I saw someone in here and didn't know it was you. I thought for a moment John Wyvern had returned."

"Wyvern? No, of course not." An annoyed expression flitted over the scientist's face. "You came to see me?"

Tom explained the urgent reason for his visit.

"Sorry. You're in the same boat I am," Kimer said. "I need one of Wyvern's activators for my own experiments, but I can't find the slightest details on how he made them. That's what I was looking for just now."

Tom's face showed his keen disappointment. "Can't you find one among his lab setups?"

Kimer shook his head. "No. It's odd, but Wyvern seems to have removed or destroyed all the activators he used in his own experiments before we left for Detroit."

The young inventor's eyes roved glumly about the laboratory. On a shelf he noticed a small, beautifully carved wooden box, bearing the name *Elsa* in raised letters on the cover.

"Does that belong to his daughter?" Tom murmured. "Perhaps I should take it to her."

Kimer came over, picked up the box, and raised

the lid. Although the box was empty, a tinkling melody began to play—apparently from a concealed Swiss-type musical mechanism.

"Probably a powder box or jewel case Wyvern was carving for her," said Kimer. "Take it along, by all means."

As Tom left the building, he met Victor Fronz, one of the Sonicon electronic engineers with whom he had spoken at the convention. They chatted, then Tom went out to the parking lot.

A green light was glowing on the dashboard radio. Tom flicked on the set and answered.

"Message for you from Harlan Ames," said the Enterprises operator. "He and that FBI agent, Wes Norris, have gone to question Phineas Gull." The operator named a small midtown hotel in New York. "Mr. Ames wants to know if you care to join them."

Tom glanced at his wristwatch. "Right! Tell him I'll be there by five-thirty."

The atomicar sped eastward through the sky to Manhattan Island. Tom managed to pick out the street and settled neatly down at the curb.

The desk clerk had been told to expect Tom. He named Gull's room number and Tom went up. Phineas Gull himself opened the door.

"Come in, come in," the writer said in a falsely hearty voice.

The wispy little man's demeanor was altogether different from the last time Tom had seen him.

Instead of being arrogant and sarcastic, he now seemed pale and frightened.

Tom greeted Ames and Wes Norris, an old friend of the Swifts. Both investigators remained on their feet while Gull huddled in a chair.

As the two went on with their grilling, Gull insisted he knew nothing of the sonic plot.

"In Detroit you sounded as if you might know a good deal about it," Tom said quietly.

The Adam's apple in Gull's scrawny neck bobbed up and down nervously. "I was just grandstanding," he mumbled. "I was hoping for some valuable publicity."

"The whole plot ought to be worth a fortune in publicity to the new edition of your book, eh?" Norris whipped out a copy of *The Sonic Invaders.*

Gull's mummylike face turned white as a sheet. "I know it seems like a funny coincidence," he whined. "But that's all it is. Maybe whoever's behind these attacks has read my book. You can't blame me for wanting to cash in on the headlines, can you?"

"A year ago you disappeared for a while," said Ames. "Why? Where did you go?"

Gull drew out a handkerchief and mopped his perspiring forehead. "I—I suffered a nervous breakdown from overwork. I had to go to a mental sanitarium. It was—well, very embarrassing—so I did my best to keep it a secret."

"We'll soon check that out!" Norris snapped. He asked for the name and location of the sanitarium, then picked up the telephone and told the operator to call the institution. A few minutes later Norris hung up, looking baffled.

"What's the word?" Ames asked.

"The local operator says the place closed down a month ago. There's just a caretaker on the premises." Norris shot a gimlet-eyed glance at Phineas Gull. "If you're trying to pull a fast one, don't think you'll get away with it. We'll trace the staff and find out the truth."

"Why wait?" Tom spoke up. "I can fly us there right now in my atomicar. If the furnishings haven't been removed, we can check their office files and see if there's any record of Mr. Gull having been a patient."

"Great!" said Ames. "But let's find a restaurant and grab a bite to eat first."

Dusk had fallen by the time Tom's atomicar was swooping down toward the mental hospital on a wooded New Jersey hillside. The buildings were enclosed within a high metal fence. Tom landed, and with his two companions strode toward a small, lighted, red-brick gatehouse.

No one answered the bell. Norris tried the door. Finding it open, he stepped inside—then stopped short and sucked in his breath.

An elderly man lay sprawled unconscious in a chair!

CHAPTER XIV

BLACK OPALS

"HE must be the caretaker!" Ames exclaimed.

There was a livid bruise on the man's temple.

"Alive, though," the FBI agent said, after checking the unconscious man's pulse. "Somebody slugged him."

Tom hastily dampened a towel in the gatehouse kitchen, then bathed the victim's forehead. After a few moments the man revived.

"Wh-who are you?" he stammered, looking up at the three people bending over him.

"Take it easy," Norris said. He flipped open his wallet to show his identification. "I'm from the Federal Bureau of Investigation—here to check on some records at the sanitarium. Suppose you tell us who *you* are and how you got kayoed."

"I'm Sam Baynes, the caretaker." The man's eyes filled with fear. "W-w-wait! I remember now. It was a masked man! I heard someone at the door. When I opened it, he jammed a gun at me and then cracked me over the head with it. I fell onto this chair."

"How about your keys?" Ames put in.

Baynes fished in his pockets. "They're gone!"

"Looks as though someone got here before us—and he may be inside the sanitarium right now!" said Norris.

Drawing his own gun, the FBI agent strode out of the gatehouse. Tom, Ames, and the caretaker followed.

Besides the main dormitory of the sanitarium, there were two smaller buildings. Baynes said one contained the heating plant and workshop; the other, the administration offices.

Norris went straight to the small office building. Its door was unlocked. Inside, he pressed a light switch. A hasty search showed that the place had been ransacked. Several drawers of one large filing cabinet, labeled "Case Histories," had been yanked open and a number of folders lay scattered on the floor.

Tom checked through the files while Ames and Norris searched the other buildings. When they returned, Tom announced grimly, "If there was any record here on Gull, it's gone."

"Tough break," said Norris. "The thief seems to have made a complete getaway. Well, that's that." After reporting the theft to the State Police over the atomicar radio, Tom and his friends flew back to Shopton.

When Mr. Swift arrived at the plant next day, he went to Tom's lab and found the young inventor hard at work. Tom was machining a small, oddly shaped cylinder on a bench lathe.

"Get any sleep last night, son?"

Tom gave a rueful grin and rubbed his hands over his eyes. "A couple of hours." He told what had happened the night before and added, "Kimer can't find any of Wyvern's activators so I've been trying to make one."

"Any luck?"

"Not yet, Dad. It's a tricky job."

Tom explained that the frequency of the liquid crystals could only be changed by varying the dimensions of their container. This required an intricately machined cylinder with a movable plunger.

"The trouble is," he went on, "the irregular shape of the cylinder walls makes it very easy to rupture by vibrational fatigue."

"I see what you mean." Mr. Swift discussed the problem, but came to no conclusions.

Later in the morning Ames called to report that neither the New Jersey police nor the FBI had found any clues to the masked man.

"Incidentally," Ames said, "Gull has a solid alibi. He probably had no way to get to the sanitarium fast enough, anyhow."

"He could have phoned a confederate."

"Sure, but how do we prove it?" Ames said

gloomily. "Another thing—the doctor who ran the sanitarium died. That's why the place closed. It may take days to trace his staff."

"And the attack deadline is only three days away—on Saturday." Tom's jaw muscles clenched. "Well, keep plugging, Harlan."

Tom worked feverishly all day and into the evening. He hardly touched the tasty supper wheeled into the lab by Chow.

Suddenly the telephone rang. It was Arv Hanson calling from Australia. His voice sounded excited. "We've finally got a clue, skipper."

"Let's hear it," Tom said.

Arv reported that he had shown Wyvern's opal to several gem experts in Sydney. One had recognized it as similar in quality to a parcel of raw black opals which had been deposited at a bank to be bid on by gem buyers.

"So I went to the bank as soon as it opened this morning," Arv went on. "The manager told me that the parcel in question had been brought in by a 'Mr. Jonson.' He figures the name was phony. It seems opal miners often cover up that way when they've made a new strike and want to keep the location a secret."

"Is Jonson coming back to the bank?"

"No, the opals were sold and he has already collected his money. But the bank manager gave me a good description of him. Jonson is wiry—very tanned as if he might have spent a lot of time in the

Outback—and has thin, dark hair and a deep pockmark on his left temple."

Tom's pulse soared. "That's great, Arv! The population of the Northern Territory is so sparse, the police should be able to run him down fast with that much to go on. And once they find him, I'll bet we find Wyvern!"

Arv said that he and Elsa were about to fly back to Alice Springs to get Sergeant Kincaid's help in tracing Jonson.

Tom reached a quick decision. "Stay put in Alice Springs, Arv," he ordered. "I'll meet you there before the day's over."

After hanging up, Tom made several hasty phone calls. One was to his father. Tom told him the news and said, "Dad, will you help me?"

"Any way possible, son. What can I do?"

"We both know the sort of electromechanical activator that's needed for these liquid crystals," Tom replied. "It's mainly a matter of testing and rejecting until we figure out the right design. But time's running out!"

"It is, indeed," Mr. Swift said gravely.

"If we could find Wyvern, he could give us the answer in a minute. Dad, if you'll take over here in the lab, I'd like to fly down and help out in the search!"

The elder Swift immediately agreed. In fifteen minutes he arrived at the laboratory. Tom showed him the various models he had tried out so far, and also the results of his computer testing of other designs.

Then the younger inventor snatched a brief nap in the apartment next to his lab. When Bud and Chow came to wake him up an hour later, the *Sky Queen* was ready to take off. Doc Simpson had also volunteered to rejoin the search.

The huge ship soon rose from the runway with a steady blast of its jet lifters. Tom napped again as the plane streaked high across the continent and out over the Pacific. Hank Sterling and Bud were at the controls.

Four hours later they were settling down on the Alice Springs airfield. Here it was already Thursday afternoon. The very thought struck Tom with a fresh pang of urgency.

Calling the hotel, he learned that Arv and Elsa had just arrived from Sydney. Tom arranged to meet them at the police station. Then he and Bud taxied into town.

Arv and Elsa greeted them warmly in Sergeant Kincaid's office. The sergeant himself gave each boy a hearty handshake.

"Welcome back, cobbers! I knew you couldn't stay away long from a place like the Alice."

Tom responded with a grin. "This time we're hoping we won't go home without John Wyvern. Have you told him your new lead yet, Arv?"

"I was just filling him in, skipper." Arv repeated the description of Mr. Jonson.

"Hmm." Sergeant Kincaid sat back with a thoughtful frown. "I've been all over the Territory and I reckon I've seen a fair share of the people on the Outback, but offhand that description doesn't ring any bells. The man should be fairly easy to recognize with that pockmark."

Elsa's face fell. "Please don't tell us this is just another false hope!" she pleaded.

"Far from it, miss. If this bloke Jonson's in the Territory, we'll run him down, no fear, but it may take a while. I'll shoot his description to all police posts—and there's also a good chance the Never-Never Mailman may know of him."

"Who's the Never-Never Mailman?" Bud asked.

"The Never-Never's another name for the Outback," Kincaid explained, "and the Never-Never Mailman's an air service that delivers mail to cattle stations all over the center and the top end of the Territory. One of the pilots may—"

A buzz from Tom's pencil radio interrupted him. Tom pulled it from his pocket and flicked on the mike. "Tom here. Come in, please."

"This is Chow, boss," said the cook's voice. "Weren't you lookin' fer a tanned, dark-haired hombre with a pockmark on his left temple?"

"Yes, we are!" Tom replied. "Why?"

"I jest been talkin' to him here at the airfield."

CHAPTER XV

ALARM SIGNAL

THE others in Sergeant Kincaid's office saw Tom's eyebrows shoot up as he heard Chow say that he had seen a man who might be Jonson.

"He's just leavin', so I can't talk any more now," the cook went on. "I aim to follow him into town an' see where he goes. You wait fer me there at the police station, boss."

Signing off, Tom reported the startling news. As they waited anxiously, Bud's glance happened to fall on a package which Tom had brought along from the *Sky Queen*.

"Forgetting something, aren't you, pal?"

Tom saw what Bud was looking at. "Oh, that's right," he said, picking up the package. "Elsa, I made a trip to Sonicon the other day and saw this in your father's lab."

Elsa undid the wrappings. Inside was the music box.

"Oh, Tom, thank you for bringing this! I'm so

glad to have it!" she said with a catch in her voice. "Dad must have made this himself."

"He sure did a beautiful job," Bud said.

"Yes, wood carving and inlay work was his hobby," Elsa said. "He mentioned in Detroit that he had something at his lab for me."

She lifted the lid. The same tinkling tune began to play that Tom had heard before—an old German song, "The Lorelei."

Tears glistened in Elsa's eyes and she hastily closed the lid again. "Dad knew that was my favorite melody," she faltered.

Twenty minutes later a roly-poly figure in a ten-gallon hat came clumping into the office.

"What's the scoop, Chow?" Tom asked.

"Jonson went into a place called the Drover's Retreat," the Texan reported.

"Why, that's the hotel where I've been staying!" Elsa spoke up.

Sergeant Kincaid immediately called the hotel and gave Jonson's description to the desk clerk. "Did a chap like that come into your place a few minutes ago, Charlie?"

The sergeant listened for a moment, then added, "Know who he is? . . . Hmm. . . . Thanks."

Hanging up, Kincaid said, "He's in the hotel dining room, getting a bite to eat. The clerk thinks he has seen him around town before but doesn't know his name."

Tom turned back to the stout cook. "Tell us how you happened to spot him, Chow."

"Wal, I was standin' there on the field, watchin' Hank check our jets when this lil ole plane landed. Fellow climbed out an' give the *Queen* a good stare an' then he sashayed over an' struck up a conversation with me. Wanted to know where we come from an' who owned her."

"Did you ask him about himself?" Tom inquired.

"I tried to, but he sort o' got lockjaw at that point an' said he had things to attend to in town. That's when I called you."

"What sort of plane does he have?" put in Sergeant Kincaid.

Chow removed his ten-gallon hat and scratched his bald dome. "Don't rightly know, Sarge, but she was a lil one-engine job—red an' white."

Again Kincaid made a telephone call—this time to the Alice Springs airfield. He spoke to the tower, then put the phone back on its cradle.

"That plane belongs to the Bildana station," he reported, "and the pilot—he's the bloke you yabbered with, Chow—is named Yunsen."

"Name's sort of close to 'Jonson,'" Arv commented.

"What is the Bildana station?" Tom asked. "A cattle ranch?"

Kincaid nodded. "A big layout. Owned by two brothers named Delperta. They're New Australians. Came here three or four years ago from some place in Eastern Europe."

"Where's their station?"

Sergeant Kincaid got up from his desk and pointed to a spot on a wall map of the Northern Territory. "It's up here near the Barkly Tableland—quite a bit north of the Murchisons."

Arv gasped. "That's one of the areas where the gem experts told us opals might possibly be found! They occur in beds of Lower Cretaceous rock—and you find that either in the southeast corner of the Territory, or else up north around the Barkly Tableland."

"It all seems to fit, Sergeant," Tom pointed out. "Even the plane. That *could* be the ship that picked up Dr. Wyvern and the men with him from the brush-fire area!"

"Too right. Suppose I have Yunsen brought in for questioning."

"No—not yet, please." Tom rose from his chair and paced tensely about the office. "Let's not tip our hand till we have more to go on. If his bosses get wind of it, that might give them time to get rid of Elsa's father—assuming they're the ones who are holding him."

"What do you suggest, cobber?"

"That we fly up and scout out their cattle station first. Meantime, Elsa, I'd like you to go back to your hotel and keep an eye on Yunsen. If he's mixed up in this business, he must know you're John Wyvern's daughter—and he may betray that somehow, from the way he acts. Let him see you, but don't take any risks. Remember, he may be a dangerous man."

Elsa agreed breathlessly to Tom's plan. "You needn't worry about me—not with Fido for a protector," she added with a smile. "Arv has converted him back into a guard dog."

"Good," Tom said. "I was counting on that."

The two boys, Arv, and Chow rode back to the airfield in a police car driven by Sergeant Kincaid. The *Sky Queen* took off and streaked northward over the barren, rust-colored Outback.

Kincaid guided Hank, who was piloting, to the Bildana station. From the air it looked much like any other cattle ranch in the Territory—a small cluster of buildings, with horse paddocks and a circular reservoir tank.

The Flying Lab settled down gently on the sun-baked ground. It was nearing the supper hour and several of the station hands, who had been loafing near the bunkhouse, came strolling out to stare at the plane. Some were white men and others were aborigines or half-castes.

Before Tom and his companions could speak to any of them, a big ruddy-faced man with a dark mustache came striding out from the main ranch building.

"Evening, gentlemen. It isn't often we get visitors. You must have some special reason for coming." He spoke with a faint foreign accent.

"That's right, sir. I'm Sergeant Kincaid of the Territorial force." The policeman introduced Tom and the other members of the party.

The rancher identified himself as Serge Delperta.

"We're looking for a friend of mine," said Tom, "an American named John Wyvern. He's lost somewhere on the Outback."

"Ah, yes. That must be the lost white man I've heard talk about." Delperta stroked his mustache. "A sign he made was sighted from the air, wasn't it? But I thought that was far south of here—down near the Murchisons."

"It was, but we've picked up some clues that indicated he might have come this way," said Kincaid. "We were hoping you or your brother or some of your men might have glimpsed him."

Delperta shrugged. "I myself can tell you nothing. My brother Otto is up at Darwin—on business. But perhaps you would like to speak to the hands."

"Thanks. We would," Kincaid said quickly.

Delperta called over his men. Tom and the sergeant questioned them, but they replied mostly with shakes of their heads. None volunteered any information. Nor did Delperta show any of the

traditional Australian hospitality by inviting his
visitors into the ranch house.

As the *Sky Queen* took off, Bud remarked,
"Pretty unsociable guy—and secretive."

"Too right," Kincaid said dryly. "I have a feeling Delperta was glad to see us go."

Tom ordered Hank to circle slowly over the cattle station before heading south again. The

young inventor snapped a series of photographs with the *Queen's* regular aerial camera.

"What's the idea?" Doc Simpson inquired.

"We can't very well hang around and spy on the place," Tom replied, "but I'm hoping these shots may show us if there's any sign of opal digging around the ranch."

The surrounding hills loomed red in the dusk when they arrived back at Alice Springs. By this time the photographs had been developed and printed. Sergeant Kincaid, Bud, and the others gathered around Tom in the lab compartment to study the results.

Suddenly they were all startled by a shrill, pulsing sound. Arv Hanson plucked a small, electronic device from his pocket.

"That's Fido's signal!" he exclaimed. "Elsa must be in trouble!"

CHAPTER XVI

A PROBE IN THE DARK

THE news of Elsa's danger sent a chill of foreboding through Tom and his companions.

"Can you tell where she is?" Sergeant Kincaid asked tensely.

"That gadget Arv's holding will home on the signal," Tom replied. "Let's go!"

He and his friends hustled out of the *Sky Queen* and piled into the police car. Kincaid threw it into gear and sped from the airfield. Almost at once a loud alarm siren became audible.

"Is that from Fido too?" Bud asked.

"Yes, and I have a hunch that dog has the situation well in hand!" Tom replied.

The whole population of Alice Springs seemed to have been aroused by the alarm. People were pouring into the streets.

The siren grew louder as the police car headed

along Gap Road, lined with tall gum trees. They passed the stone gateway to Traeger Park. Farther ahead the darkness was lit up by a brilliant white glow, but the source of the light was hidden by a cluster of excited people.

Kincaid braked to a screeching halt as they reached the scene. The knot of onlookers gave way, revealing an amazing sight.

A man was half-sitting, half-lying on the ground near Elsa and Fido. A powerful, springlike tendril from the electronic watchdog's jaws was coiled around one leg of the man, who was gripping the tendril with both hands and seemed unable to let go.

He raised his head with a look of snarling hatred as Tom's group climbed out of the police car. A pockmark could be seen on his left temple in the glare from Fido's collar lights.

"Yunsen—alias Jonson!" Arv exclaimed.

"The blighter's caught fast!" spoke up one of the spectators. "That ruddy robot trapped him when he tried to annoy the young lady!"

The speaker had to shout to make himself heard. Tom hastily flicked a switch on Fido, shutting off the siren. Elsa, still pale and trembling, told what had happened.

"He tried to make me go with him—he said he'd take me to my father." She pointed to a car parked nearby in the shadow of the trees. "When I refused, he got rough and threatened me. In the darkness I don't think he noticed Fido following me. But I did what you said, Tom, and pressed the stone in my cameo ring. After that, everything seemed to happen at once."

Instantly the lights on Fido's collar had flashed on, Elsa related, then the alarm siren had gone off. As the robot had rolled forward to attack, a tube had shot out of its jaws and coiled around Yunsen's leg. When the man tried to yank it off, a gluey foam had oozed out of the tubing, gripping the skin of his hands with a powerful adhesive force.

"She's lying!" Yunsen snarled. "I never even spoke to her! For no reason at all, she sicced this blasted robot on me!"

"You're wasting your breath," Tom retorted. "For your information, Fido's eyes are actually television camera lenses. Everything that happened was recorded on video tape."

Bud burst into hoots of laughter at the look of dismay that spread over Yunsen's face.

Chow guffawed. "Brand my chuck wagon, that Fido's better'n a shotgun guard! I take back all the ornery things I ever said about the critter, boss. I'd like to feed him a T-bone steak!"

"We knew he was a swell bloodhound," Bud added, patting the automaton's head, "but this proves he's the best rathound in the business!"

Tom explained that Fido had been guided to

the assailant by an infrared sensor and photo-scanning system which were activated when Elsa had pressed the stone in her ring.

Sergeant Kincaid shoved back his hat and scratched his head. "How do we get this fellow loose, Tom—or do we take him in as is?"

"Bring Yunsen out to the airfield," Tom said. "I have a chemical aboard the Flying Lab that will dissolve the adhesive on his hands."

The prisoner was loaded into the back seat of the police car with his robot captor. Chow volunteered to accompany the sergeant as he started back to the airfield. Tom, Elsa, and the others followed in Yunsen's car, which they learned later he had rented in town.

On the way, Tom asked Elsa how the encounter with Yunsen had come about. She explained that she had sat in the hotel lobby reading a magazine in order to see what the suspect might do.

"When he came out of the dining room, I was sure he had noticed me," she went on. "But he didn't try to speak or sit by me. Instead, he left the hotel. I decided I'd better not follow him."

"Smart girl," Tom approved.

"Then, just about twilight, I got a telephone call," Elsa said.

"From whom?" Bud asked.

"The caller wouldn't give any name—and he sounded frightened, as if he was taking his life in his hands just by getting in touch with me. It was very realistic and convincing! He begged me not to tell anyone, but said if I would meet him near the park, he could give me some important information about my father."

Elsa said her instructions were to take a taxi to the park gates, then walk along the road in the direction away from town.

"I knew it was dangerous," Elsa confessed. "But I was willing to take the risk if it might help us find Dad—and besides, I was sure Fido would protect me."

Aboard the Flying Lab, Tom applied a chemical solvent which loosened Yunsen's hands from the electronic dog. The turn of a switch on Fido uncoiled the tube from his leg. Next, Tom ran the video tape through a televiewer. The picture sequence clearly bore out Elsa's story of the attempted kidnapping.

"Now then, mate," Sergeant Kincaid advised Yunsen, "you'd better start talking."

Yunsen's deeply tanned face had gone sickly pale. His eyes moved about shiftily with the look of a cornered rat. But he seemed even more fearful of squealing on his criminal pals than of going to prison.

"I've got nothing to tell you," he whined.

The handcuffed prisoner was taken away by two policemen whom the sergeant had summoned. Tom resumed his study of the aerial photographs.

"Hang it all, I can't find the slightest sign of any opal digging," he told Kincaid.

"Maybe Wyvern didn't pick up that opal at the ranch," Bud put in.

"You might be right. But one thing's sure—if Yunsen sold a parcel of opals, his gang must have been digging somewhere."

"Mebbe them owlhoots have some other hideout where they're holdin' Wyvern," Chow suggested.

"It's possible," Tom agreed, "but the Outback's so barren, any kind of a setup would mean a risk of attracting attention—whereas the ranch makes a perfect cover."

The young inventor paced about the lab compartment. Suddenly he stopped and snapped his fingers. "Wait a second! Infrared photography may give us the answer!"

"What'll that do?" Sergeant Kincaid inquired.

"If there are any underground diggings or tunnels at Bildana, the difference in ground temperature will make them show up perfectly on infrared film!"

In minutes the *Sky Queen* was circling slowly and silently in the darkness, high above the cattle station while a camera clicked off pictures. Then it streaked back to Alice Springs.

Tom was jubilant as he studied the results. *The infrared film showed the grounds about the ranch to be honeycombed with an elaborate tunnel system!*

"That's not just a mine!" he exclaimed. "There's a lot more going on at the Bildana station than cattle raising *or* opal gouging!"

"Genius boy, I think you've solved a mystery!" Bud exclaimed.

Plans were hastily laid. Later Sergeant Kincaid's big fist pounded loudly on the front door of the ranch house. When Serge Delperta opened it, he found himself facing the sergeant and Tom Swift.

"Rather late for a visit, isn't it, Sergeant?" the rancher said, obviously stalling.

Kincaid held out a paper. "This is a warrant, authorizing us to search the ground and premises on the suspicion that you may be holding John Wyvern a prisoner."

Delperta's expression froze. He stood aside from the doorway while the two entered.

"You can save time by showing us the entrance to your underground system," Tom told him.

"I'm sorry you found out about that," said the rancher softly. "Now neither of you will leave this place alive!"

As he spoke, Delperta raised his hand, displaying a strange-looking weapon!

CHAPTER XVII

THE BRAIN TWISTERS

"THIS device I'm holding fires small needles of instant anesthetic," Delperta told Tom and Kincaid. "Shall I prove it? Or will you both raise your hands sensibly and surrender?"

Tom and the sergeant exchanged dismayed looks but obeyed. Delperta roared with laughter.

"Did you really expect to take me unawares, my dear Swift? I've been expecting you back ever since your earlier visit this evening."

"Is that why you ordered Yunsen to kidnap Elsa Wyvern?" Tom asked.

"Quite right. He communicated with me by radio soon after you left here," said Delperta. "If you've captured him, it makes no difference. He will never talk—that I guarantee."

"What makes you so sure?" Kincaid spoke up.

Delperta's ruddy face took on an evil grin. "My

brother and I have ways—scientific ways—of insuring that our employees will not betray us. Furthermore, I was warned by my men the moment your plane prepared to land."

"There are half a dozen people aboard that plane," Tom said. "What about them?"

Delperta's grin became even wider. "One of you will go and ask them to join us. And your reason had better sound convincing. If the plane tries to take off, my men in the bunkhouse are ready to blast it with bazookas."

"You seem to have thought of everything."

"I try." Delperta smirkingly stroked his mustache. "Eventually your plane will be found crashed and burned—an unfortunate accident on your way back to Alice Springs."

"Then our hunch was correct," Tom said. "You *are* holding Wyvern here somewhere?"

"Too right, my friend. He's down below in a most interesting laboratory-prison which you will see shortly. But we are wasting time. I fear I must now summon my assistants."

Delperta reached out toward a bell button. He paused at the sound of a commotion outdoors.

"What's going on out there?" he snarled.

"Take a look," Tom said, and gave a sudden, piercing whistle.

Instantly the blaze of the *Sky Queen's* giant searchlight flooded the ranch-house windows! Delperta was still gaping in confusion when the door burst open. In strode several police and men of the Royal Australian Air Force! Two of them seized the stunned rancher.

"Three planeloads of airmen and police were closing in on this place before we ever landed," Kincaid told him. "It was Tom Swift's idea to keep you occupied during the mop-up, so you'd have no chance to use Wyvern as a hostage."

"Incidentally, your brother has already been arrested in Darwin," Tom added.

"The hands in the bunkhouse have been subdued, sir," one policeman reported to Sergeant Kincaid. "Quite an arsenal they had. But they caved in fast when they saw the odds."

Delperta gave a wry shrug. "I am no fool, either," he said. "I think it will go much better for me if I assist you from here on."

"Now you're talking sense," Kincaid replied.

Serge Delperta led them down a flight of steps to the underground tunnel system. Below was a maze of corridors and rooms.

Some of the rooms appeared to be outfitted as medical and psychological laboratories. Three white-jacketed attendants gave up at once.

Other rooms had black, specially baffled walls designed to shut out all sights and sounds except those fed in by projection equipment. Beyond these were barred cells containing dazed, zombie-like prisoners.

"What kind of a horror-camp setup have you

The police officers seized the rancher

been running here?" Kincaid demanded furiously.

"An elaborate kidnapping and brainwashing racket, I imagine," said Tom Swift.

Delperta confessed that he and his brother had masterminded a worldwide kidnap ring which specialized in seizing top scientists and government officials. The victims were flown to a small jungle island off the Australian coast and then smuggled into the Territory by his brother. Here they were brainwashed to extract their secrets by techniques which the Delpertas had learned in a totalitarian country. The secrets were sold to foreign powers or unscrupulous industrial firms. Then the victims were returned home with all memory of what had happened blanked out.

"We did them no harm," Delperta defended himself.

"Aside from the mind-warping you inflicted on them!" Tom snapped back in a cold, angry voice. "Where's John Wyvern?"

"In this next cell down the corridor."

As they entered, they saw the sandy-haired scientist lying cringingly on his cot. He was cleanly clothed and shaven, but his eyes were as full of fear as ever. He replied only in low mumbles when Tom and the sergeant tried to talk to him.

Delperta explained that after being brought to the ranch, Wyvern had escaped by hiding in the back of a truck that was being driven to the town of Tennant Creek for supplies. En route the driver had discovered him, but Wyvern had fled.

Later, the criminals had heard a radio report of his sign for help and had tried desperately to find him before the police did. One of Delperta's aborigine workers had speared Ben.

After Wyvern was found, three of Delperta's men seized him from the cave. Yunsen had picked them up by plane. As Tom suspected, the bush fire had been set to cover their getaway.

"I fear the hardships Wyvern suffered on the Outback, added to the partial brainwashing he received earlier, have affected his mind," said Delperta.

Even the sight of Elsa, who had come along aboard the *Queen,* did nothing to restore Wyvern's memory.

"Treatment by tranquillizers may help," said Doc Simpson. "But, offhand, I'd say it may be days or weeks before he's back to normal."

The news dealt a blow to Tom's hopes. Now there was no chance of getting technical data on Wyvern's activator before the sonic attack deadline.

"How did you happen to pick Wyvern as a victim?" he asked Delperta.

"It was a special job. We were hired to kidnap him."

"What! Hired by whom?"

Delperta shrugged. "I do not know. One of our

agents in New York was contacted secretly. We were offered a high price to kidnap Wyvern and brainwash him to their specifications."

"What does that mean?" put in Bud.

"He was to be turned into a will-less slave who would use his technical skill in any way to serve his masters. We were to receive instructions later on where to deliver him."

"Have you heard from these people since the kidnapping?" Tom asked.

"My brother in Darwin talked with them several days ago by radio," Delperta replied. "He had to tell them we were having no success."

"And you have no idea who they are?"

Delperta shook his head. "They identified themselves only by the password 'sonic.' "

"*Sonic!*" Bud exclaimed. "Jumpin' jets! They may be the sonic attackers!"

Tom nodded grimly. "Could be they tried to hire him first but he refused. Maybe that's what he wanted to discuss with me in Detroit before he was kidnapped."

Tom radioed a full report of the night's events to Swift Enterprises. By now a pink flush of dawn was paling the sky over the Outback, but in Shopton it was still late afternoon of the previous day. Mr. Swift was as horrified to learn of Wyvern's condition as Tom had been.

"What about the activator, Dad?" Tom went on. "Any progress?"

"Right now I seem to be up against a stone wall. I had a promising idea which involved freezing the crystals. But the technical difficulties with the materials I've been testing for the container seem almost insurmountable." Tom signed off, deep in gloom.

Meanwhile, the police and R.A.A.F. personnel had been dealing with their prisoners and the victims rescued from the underground cells.

"We still haven't found out how the opals figured in this setup," Arv remarked.

Delperta explained that while excavating the underground tunnels, his men had struck a rich vein of opal-bearing rock. Yunsen had been detailed to sell the gems in Sydney.

It was broad daylight by the time the *Sky Queen* took off on the return flight to America. Tom, goaded by worry over the looming sonic attack, was unable to rest and spent the entire trip at the controls.

When the huge ship landed in Shopton, it was still Thursday evening. Ames and Mr. Swift were on hand to greet them.

"We're still checking out Phineas Gull's story, skipper," Ames began, "but so far we—"

He stopped as a strange look came over Tom's face. Suddenly the young inventor collapsed to the ground!

CHAPTER XVIII

ZERO HOUR!

AMID anxious exclamations, Doc Simpson crouched down and examined Tom.

"Just a case of complete exhaustion," the medic said. "He's been on the go for so long that nature took over and blanked him out. All he needs now is a good long sleep."

"Thank heavens it's nothing worse," Mr. Swift murmured.

Bud and Arv helped to lift Tom into a jeep. His father supported him while Bud drove to Tom's laboratory. Here the young inventor was put to bed in the adjoining apartment.

When Tom awoke hours later, sunshine was pouring in the windows. A glance at his wristwatch showed it was 10:24. Then he saw Bud grinning at him from a nearby chair.

Tom kicked off the covers. "How'd I get here?" he exclaimed. "What day is this?"

"Easy, boy. One question at a time," Bud said. "You conked out on the airstrip. It's now Friday morning and high time for some bacon and eggs. What say?"

Tom gave a dazed nod. "Wow! I must've slept the clock around."

"You did and then some." Bud stepped to a wall intercom and buzzed the galley. "Chow down, fat stuff! Genius boy just came to."

Chuckling at Chow's retort, Bud looked back at Tom. The young inventor's forehead was creased with worry. "What's wrong, pal?"

"Friday morning—just one day left—and my Silentenna is still a flop. Bud, I've really let everyone down this time!"

"The blitz hasn't hit yet, so cut out the gloom. Confidentially, I think your dad may have some news for you."

A brisk shower made the world look somewhat brighter to Tom. As he was finishing brunch, his father strode into the apartment.

"Well! Back in top form, I see, Tom."

"Sure! Fit as ever, Dad. But we're really going to have to work on that activator."

Mr. Swift reached into the pocket of his tweed jacket. "I think our problem's solved."

The scientist pulled out a small device made of a glistening white material. It was approximately cylindrical with irregular outer walls and wire leads at each end. An intricate lengthwise coil arrangement was connected to the cylinder by a pair of metal collars.

"Made of Durastress, isn't it?" Tom queried. This was a plastic of amazing strength which he had invented to incase the midget atomic power plant in his flying atomicars.

"Yes, and it never came in handier. I discovered how to cast it to a ten-thousandth tolerance with the liquid crystals frozen inside. Using the Durastress completely eliminated any machining or polishing."

Mr. Swift said he had worked all night before finding a solution. "Varying the potential over the coil changes the size of the crystal, causing it to slide right and left over a central tube—thus varying the frequency."

"Dad, this is terrific! I'll bet it's superior to Wyvern's model!"

"Hank Sterling has a crew turning out a whole batch of these," Mr. Swift added.

Tom rushed into his laboratory and set to work at once. Within the next few hours he made the necessary changes in his Silentenna.

First he converted both the large twin-unit model and the smaller model salvaged from Lake Carlopa. Both tested out perfectly.

"Nice going," said Bud. "What's the next step? Another flight test?"

Tom shook his head. "Not yet. First I want to check this new gear in a city environment."

"Like for instance?"

"You know that stretch on Prospect Street in Shopton that's being torn up?" Tom said. "Well, that should give us a real check-out."

The two boys loaded the small Silentenna unit into a panel truck and sped into town. Tom swung over to the curb on Prospect Street near a jack-hammer crew who were busily ripping up the concrete paving. The din was deafening.

"Man, if you can silence this racket, you'll have it made!" Bud shouted into his pal's ear.

Tom grinned, got out, and opened up the rear door of the truck. Then he switched on power to the Silentenna.

As if by magic, the street was instantly blanketed in silence!

Tom hastily climbed back into the cab. In a moment both boys were doubled up with laughter. Pedestrians stood staring around in amazement. The workmen gaped open-mouthed at the pneumatic drills vibrating noiselessly in their hands.

The workers tried turning their machines on and off, as if they could not believe what was happening. Two ran to the foreman. All three began exclaiming wildly, and became even more frantic when not a word came from their mouths.

Several bystanders had noticed the Swift Enterprises truck and pointed to it. The foreman ran over to speak to the two boys.

Tom climbed out and switched off the device. Then he picked up the small electric bullhorn he had brought along and spoke to the crowd:

"Ladies and gentlemen, I'm sorry if what happened just now startled you. I was testing a new invention to blank out sounds."

Almost every American citizen knew by this time of the threatened sonic attack. It was also known that the Swifts had been called in by the Pentagon to help cope with the danger. As a result, many people in the crowd guessed at once that the device Tom had been testing was intended for this purpose. They broke into loud cheers and applause.

Suddenly Bud noticed a light flashing on their dashboard short-wave radio. He switched it on.

"Is Tom there?" Ames's voice asked.

"Sure. Right next to me. Just a second."

Tom took the mike. "What's up, Harlan?"

"Important news from Washington, skipper! You're needed back here immediately!"

"Roger! I'm on my way!"

Tom's foot trod heavily on the gas pedal as the truck raced back to the experimental station. At the Main Building, Miss Trent informed Tom, "Your father and Mr. Ames are waiting in the office."

The faces of the two men were grave as Mr. Swift said, "Our government has just received a new ultimatum from the sonic attackers. The previous deadline, which would have expired tomorrow, has been canceled."

"You mean the attack is off?" Bud burst out.

"No, the deadline has been moved up. Our government now has one hour to issue an announcement that the ten million will be paid. If not, the sonic blitz will be unleashed!"

"The target is still unnamed," Ames added.

Tom and Bud were thunderstruck by the news. "No reason given why?" Tom asked.

Ames shook his head. "It may be that they got wind of what happened in Australia. My hunch is they'll want the money paid into a secret numbered bank account in Switzerland or Beirut. But they're not tipping their hand until the last possible moment."

The telephone gave a shrill ring.

"That may be Washington now," said Mr. Swift. "The Secretary of Defense was to call back."

He answered, then gave the instrument to Tom. As expected, the caller was the Secretary of Defense. "This looks like the showdown, Tom," he said tensely. "What's the status of your Silentenna? Do you think your invention's capable of meeting an all-out sonic attack?"

Tom's face was pale. He could feel his heart throbbing. "Yes, sir. My invention's ready and I think—I *hope*—that it can cope with such an attack."

"Good! Then there'll be no yielding to this blackmail threat!"

Tom plunged at once into feverish preparations. The *Sky Queen* was rolled out of its underground hangar, and the big twin-unit Silentenna was mounted under its wings.

Tom watched the minute hand of his watch breathlessly. The hour's deadline passed. Then Ames came racing to the airstrip in a jeep.

"New York's being attacked, skipper!"

In moments the *Queen* roared aloft. Half a dozen Whirling Duck helijets followed, manned by Hank Sterling, Arv Hanson, and other expert pilot-technicians. Tom's heart was thudding like a trip-hammer as the Flying Lab streaked eastward through the late-afternoon sky.

"The rats struck just at the rush hour," murmured Bud. "Boy, can you imagine what's happening to traffic there right now!"

Tom's imagination was already working all too vividly. A sickening fear clutched the pit of his stomach as he thought of the teeming population of New York City whose safety now depended on him and his invention.

As the *Queen* approached the Hudson River, the first shrill waves of sound reached the boys' ears. Its piercing intensity made Tom and Bud blanch. In the panoramic view below, they could see lines of cars jammed bumper to bumper on the George Washington Bridge and a tremendous backup of traffic outside the tunnel entrances to Manhattan.

The scene became more chaotic as the ship descended over Manhattan Island. In the canyoned streets between the rows of skyscrapers was a snarled maelstrom of cars, buses, and other vehicles. Dense crowds of panic-stricken pedestrians were fighting their way along the pavements. The sheer volume of high-pitched, wailing sound stunned the boys' senses.

"Am I seeing things?" Bud wondered.

It almost seemed as if the Empire State Building and other lofty towers were swaying and vibrating under the torrential blast.

Tom switched on his Silentenna and tuned the controls, then held his breath. The din of sound seemed to lessen, but only slightly.

Bud shot him a terrified glance. "What's wrong, Tom? Isn't the Silentenna working?"

CHAPTER XIX

SCREAMING MEEMIES

"I DON'T KNOW, Bud. It's a cinch my invention isn't having much effect!"

Tom's heart sank as the shrieking sound waves continued to blast the city. His trembling fingers worked the controls. All at once the volume of sound fell off sharply, then more.

"You're turning the trick!" Bud yelled excitedly. "You've licked the sonic attack! What made the difference?"

"The attackers are using a 'mix' of frequencies," Tom explained. "At first the Silentenna was just responding to a single dominant frequency, but now I've broadened the band. I have to keep the sounds partly audible so the emitters can be traced."

Radio flashes soon began coming in from the police and Civil Defense units. They reported the situation easing, now that the sounds had been reduced to a bearable level. Efforts were under way to unsnarl the massive traffic jams, and cars with loudspeakers were being sent all over the city to spread the calming news that the sonic attack was under control.

Tom was far more interested in reports being radioed in by his own helijets. These craft, using directional equipment and sound-measuring devices, were hovering over Manhattan trying to pinpoint the source of the sonic waves.

"Looks as though there is no single source, skipper," Hank Sterling reported. "There must be a number of sound emitters scattered around the city. And they're moving!"

"Moving?" Bud flashed a puzzled glance.

"Probably part of the attack plan, to keep them from being tracked down," Tom conjectured.

Just then Arv, cruising above Lower Manhattan, radioed, "The sounds seem to be moving south, skipper—toward Staten Island!"

"Over water!" Bud exclaimed. "Boy, this is getting weirder than ever!"

Other helijets reported that the sounds were moving outward in all directions, away from Manhattan—toward New Jersey, the Bronx, and Long Island.

"Keep after them!" Tom urged.

Suddenly Hank's excited voice came over the radio: "We've spotted one of the sound emitters!"

"What's it like?" Tom asked breathlessly.

"Small—about the size of a grapefruit. Three little rotors. It's flying like a copter . . . I'm going to ram it, skipper!"

There were confused noises. Then the voice of Hank's crewmate broke in, "We nailed it! The gadget is falling over the Jersey Meadows!"

Minutes later, Hank radioed that they had retrieved the device from the marshy area.

"Hey! The sounds are dying out!" Bud cried out as Hank's message ended.

"The attackers must have heard Hank's broadcast," Tom said, "so they turned the gadgets off to keep any more from being spotted."

Presently Hank's helijet rendezvoused with the *Sky Queen* over Manhattan. Hank climbed down a rope ladder into the Flying Lab. He handed Tom the captured sound emitter.

"So this is what those screaming meemies look like!" Bud exclaimed.

Having landed on soft, mushy ground, the object was little damaged. Tom was amazed as he disassembled the device.

"Man alive! This thing is really a masterpiece of miniaturization! It even has a small, built-in radar to avoid obstacles."

"It was radio-controlled, eh?" Bud asked.

"Right." Tom traced out its guidance and steering systems. "I'll bet this packs enough power to stay airborne for more than a day."

As he probed into the small but tremendously powerful sound generator, Tom's jaw dropped open in a look of utter astonishment.

"What's wrong, skipper?" Hank inquired.

"It has a liquid-crystal activator!"

"Like John Wyvern was working on?"

"It could be the same as Wyvern's," Tom said. "They may have forced more data out of him by brainwashing than Delperta let on. Anyhow, this sure explains why they wanted his technical know-how! They needed a flock of these for their flying sound emitters."

"But their first sonic attack was carried out at the same time Wyvern was kidnapped," Bud pointed out. "What were they using then?"

Before Tom could reply, the intercom buzzed. Ames was reported calling from Enterprises.

Tom switched on the compartment radio. "Hi, Harlan! What's up?"

"I hear you've licked the sonic attack. Great work, skipper! We may have turned up a clue right here in Shopton."

"Let's hear it!" Tom said eagerly.

"Elsa Wyvern just phoned me from your house," Ames replied. "She has discovered something which may have an important bearing on the sonic attack plot."

"She didn't say what it was?"

"No, but she's bringing it right over to the plant. I thought I should let you know."

"Glad you did, Harlan." Tom hastily told the security man about the liquid-crystal activator which he had found in the "screaming meemy." He added, "Since the sonic attack seems to be over, maybe I'd better come back there and take a look at Elsa's clue."

Signing off, Tom told Hank Sterling to take command of the *Sky Queen*. Then Tom and Bud sped back to Shopton in Hank's helijet.

Elsa was waiting in Ames's office.

"What's the clue?" Tom asked.

"It could blow this case wide open!" Ames said. He gave Tom a handwritten note. It read:

Dear Elsa:

I don't want to alarm you unnecessarily, but I shall leave this note just in case.

If anything should happen to me, tell the police to check up on Victor Fronz and Arthur Gammon at Sonicon. I suspect they're engaged in some criminal plot, but as yet I have no real information or proof.

Love,

Dad

Tom gave a whistle and passed the note to Bud. "Where'd you get this, Elsa?"

The red-haired girl held up the Swiss music box. "Do you remember how I couldn't bear to hear the melody? Well, this afternoon I let it play all the way through. As it finished, a little panel opened in the side of the box and that note popped out!"

Bud exclaimed, "Your father must have rigged that so no one would discover the note but you!"

Tom agreed. "This may explain why he wanted to talk to me in Detroit. He probably wanted to discuss his suspicions of Fronz and Gammon. A hasty accusation that he couldn't prove might have wrecked his career at Sonicon."

"But the crooks realized he was going to spill the beans, so they had him kidnapped!" Bud put in.

"The note could also explain that liquid-crystal activator you found," Ames told Tom.

"Right, Harlan. Fronz and Gammon probably stole all the activators Wyvern had made. That's why Kimer couldn't find any."

While Ames telephoned the news to Wes Norris of the FBI, Tom paced the floor.

"If those two *are* guilty," he mused, "it's a cinch they wouldn't dare use the Sonicon labs as a base for their attack on New York."

"How do we locate their setup?" Bud asked.

Tom snapped his fingers. "That screaming meemy could give us the answer, Bud!"

"How come?"

"Those gadgets are probably scattered around on the tops of buildings where no one will spot them. Radar guidance could do that. My hunch is the attackers are waiting to call them home under cover of darkness—and they're gambling that the captured meemy was too damaged to respond."

Bud's eyes glinted with excitement. "I get it! You fix up the gadget, then we let it take off on signal and follow it!"

"You read me right, fly-boy!"

In an hour the meemy's slight damages had been repaired. The boys jeeped the device out to the Enterprises airfield, where their Whirling Duck stood ready.

By this time dusk had fallen over the plant. Ames jeeped out to the airstrip with a message. "Wes Norris flew to Sonicon, but Fronz and Gammon weren't there. Dr. Kimer says they didn't show up for work today. Both were out of town also at the time of the sonic attacks on San Francisco and Atlanta!"

"Sounds as if they're the men we're after," Tom said grimly. "Keep your fingers crossed, Harlan, and let's hope my hunch pays off!"

Tom and Bud climbed aboard the helijet and waited. Their eyes remained fixed on the captured sound emitter, which lay on the runway.

As the darkness deepened, the meemy's three small rotors suddenly whirred into action. The device soared aloft into the night sky!

"Here goes!" Tom muttered through clenched teeth. He sent the helijet racing in pursuit.

Tom sent the helijet racing in pursuit

Tom had installed a tiny short-range radio-signaling device to help track it.

"The thing's heading east," Bud murmured.

At last they sighted the moonlit waters of the Hudson River. The meemy descended gracefully toward a wooded hill.

Bud snatched up a pair of binoculars. "There's a radar dish down there! And a radio tower. Some kind of building, too."

Hoping that the helijet had not been detected, Tom kept his radio silent to avoid betraying their presence. He landed in a field and the boys approached the hillside on foot.

A small, dirt service lane led upward through the trees. A sign said:

Private Road

RADIO TELEMETRY DEVICES, INC.

** Serving America's Space Age **

Bud gave a derisive snort. "Neat cover-up!"

Tom said, "We'd better watch our step. There might be some sort of detection device."

"I'm game if you are," Bud told him dryly.

The two youths climbed the hillside cautiously. Atop it stood a low brick building, bearing an RTD, INC. sign and surmounted by the two antennas Bud had spotted.

The building was dark and silent. Tom and Bud walked up to it and tried the door.

"It's open!" Tom whispered. Had it been left unlocked carelessly—or as a trap?

"Let's take a chance!" Bud urged.

They went inside. Tom shone his small pocket flashlight. They were in the central corridor of what seemed to be an ordinary office building, with glassed-in cubicles on either side. They tiptoed forward. At the end of the corridor was a door labeled "Research Laboratories."

As Tom pushed the door open, fluorescent lights flickered into brilliance—apparently switched on automatically.

Ahead lay a long room. It was full of workbenches and lab equipment, with smaller work spaces partitioned off from the main room.

"Let's give this place a quick once-over," Tom said. "Then we'll go back and call Ames."

The boys split up to probe the various cubicles. Tom had examined one and was stepping into another when he came face to face with a tall, silver-haired man. *Arthur Gammon!*

The engineer was as startled as Tom. He had apparently come up a stairwell at the rear of the cubicle. "Maybe," Tom thought, "to find out why the lights came on in the lab."

He saw Gammon's mouth open to yell. Tom moved like lightning. He sprang at the man, clapping a hand over his lips to stifle any outcry!

The two grappled fiercely. Gammon jerked his head free and screamed. Instantly the lights went out, leaving the area in pitch darkness!

Tom and Gammon traded short, vicious blows.

Tom felt something hard crack against the side of his head, stunning him momentarily. In that moment Gammon pulled away and darted off.

Tom stood for a moment, panting and trying to get his bearings in the darkness. Suddenly he became aware of a weird silence. *Tom had not even heard Gammon's running footsteps!*

Then he became aware of something else—a strange pulsing, hissing sound. "It's the blood in my eardrums!" Tom thought with a gasp.

With the sound came an unpleasant, oppressive feeling—a feeling of increased pressure as if he were dropping in an airplane.

Tom had undergone such sensations before. They were similar to what one felt in an anechoic chamber—a "dead room" designed to absorb or baffle-out all sounds. "Someone must have turned on a Silentenna!" he realized.

Instinctively Tom tried to shout for Bud. Not a sound came from his lips! A desperate feeling swept over him. How could he find his chum with no sounds to guide him?

The two boys were trapped in total darkness— at the mercy of the sonic attackers!

CHAPTER XX

THE SONIC CELL

TOM fought down a rising panic. Somehow he and Bud must find each other and escape— quickly, before their enemies could take any action.

But which way to turn? The lab area was windowless, and not even a faint glimmer relieved the pitch blackness.

"Better find the partition first," Tom thought. With the walls to guide him, he might feel his way back toward the door to the laboratories. "Here's hoping Bud does the same!"

Tom stretched out his hands and groped his way blindly until he touched a wooden surface—the wall of the cubicle. So far, so good! "Now if I can just—"

Tom broke off with a gasp as he felt himself clutched from behind! At least two pairs of hands were gripping him. A wild struggle ensued. Tom was thrown to the floor and bound hand and foot with cords.

The whole furious battle had taken place in complete silence!

Minutes went by as Tom writhed in the darkness. At last the lights went on. Tom stared around, blinking like an owl. He saw Bud being marched across the long laboratory room, wrists tied behind his back.

Victor Fronz and Arthur Gammon were following closely, evidently prodding him with some sort of weapons. The husky young flier looked tousled and battered.

Fronz flicked a wall switch, and the normal level of background sounds returned.

"You not only stole Wyvern's activators—you've also copied my Silentenna, I suppose," Tom gritted as the two engineers came closer.

Fronz chuckled. "I studied and photographed your Mark I before I sabotaged it in Detroit. We now have several installed around this building to muffle our sonic experiments."

"And in case you're wondering how we located you two in the darkness," Gammon taunted, "it was simple—with infrared snooperscopes."

"What're we supposed to do—applaud?"

Bud's furious retort drew a sneer from Gammon. "Far from it. You two punks will soon be screaming for mercy!" He and Fronz exchanged sly looks and burst into laughter.

"You made a big mistake, Swift, poking your nose into this place," Fronz said. "I suppose you tracked one of our sound emitters, eh?"

"Guess," Tom said coldly.

Fronz cuffed him. "You'll cooperate soon enough—after a slight dose of sonic torture!"

Fronz cut the cords from Tom's ankles. Then he tugged the young inventor to his feet and prodded him with a knife.

"Get going, Swift—down those stairs!"

Fronz followed close behind. Bud and his captor also descended the flight of steps.

Below lay a large, oblong room crammed with electronic gear and racks of tools. At one end, facing three bucket seats, was a huge control board studded with dials, switches, and scopes. Tom guessed that this was the control center for their attack on New York.

At the other end of the room was a steel-walled compartment with a latched door and a small, thick-paned window. Tom guessed its purpose. His jaw tightened in an effort not to betray a feeling of fear.

"Inside, you two!" Fronz ordered.

Tom and Bud entered, and the door slammed shut. The room was bare. Its inner, like its outer, walls were of smooth metal.

"What's the deal?" Bud murmured tensely.

"Some sort of sonic test chamber, I imagine. Now they intend to use it as a sonic torture cell."

Tom pointed to a series of louvered openings. "Those are probably the sound outlets."

Bud's face paled. To the boys' surprise, however, nothing seemed to happen.

"What're they waiting for?" Bud muttered.

"Search me."

The minutes dragged by. Suddenly a face with horn-rimmed spectacles and cloudy gray eyes peered in at them.

Tom gasped. "Olaf Kimer!"

The cell was opened. Kimer stood in the doorway, with Fronz and Gammon behind him.

"So we meet again, my dear Tom Swift!"

"What's the meaning of this, Dr. Kimer?"

"I should think that would be quite clear," Kimer replied with a mocking grin. "You thwarted our sonic blitz on New York City. Now you'll pay for your interference."

"So you're the real mastermind behind the sonic blackmail plot!" Tom exclaimed.

"Correct. A plot that would have netted us ten million except for your blasted Silentenna!" Kimer's face twisted into a snarl.

"Then our suspicions of Phineas Gull were all wrong?" Tom went on, stalling for time.

"As a matter of fact, it was Gull's book that gave me the idea for the sonic attack. After the convention I checked his background and realized he would make an excellent suspect to divert the attention of the FBI."

Kimer said he had assigned Gammon to keep an eye on the science-fiction writer. After learning of Gull's press-tour visit, Kimer had come to Enterprises to plant the gold watch.

When Gull checked into the New York hotel, Gammon tapped his phone. Kimer himself had eavesdropped on the radio message to Tom saying Gull was about to be grilled. He alerted Gammon, who monitored the call to the sanitarium and warned his boss that Gull might be cleared. To prevent this, Kimer had sped to the sanitarium, slugged the caretaker, and removed Gull's record from the files.

"What about John Wyvern?" Tom asked.

"His liquid-crystal activators were most useful. Unfortunately he overheard some careless remarks by Fronz and Gammon." Kimer chuckled. "The fool came and told me. I scoffed at his suspicions. But the risk that he might talk was too great, so I arranged to have him kidnapped by the Delpertas' gang."

Kimer said that he had learned of the gang's setup when he acted as go-between in the purchase of certain valuable industrial secrets by a firm which he served as consultant.

"Why did you have Wyvern brainwashed?" Tom asked. "You already had his activators."

"True. But they were fragile and ruptured easily from vibrational fatigue. In fact, we used up our whole supply in that first sonic blitz on

Detroit. We needed Wyvern's technical skill to make more. Without him, we were forced to waste days in slowly copying his activators as best we could, for each new blitz."

"And you were behind those attacks on Elsa and myself," Tom went on.

"Naturally—to make sure your new Silentenna would never be perfected and used to stop our attacks. Wyvern is also partly to blame."

Tom stared in surprise. "How so?"

"He tried to frighten the kidnappers by saying that he had already passed the word to someone about his suspicions of Fronz and Gammon. He may have been bluffing, of course—"

"It was no bluff." Tom told of the note Elsa had discovered in the music box.

Kimer scowled. "At any rate, I suspected he was referring to you or Elsa."

Kimer said he had hoped to get rid of them both by blowing up the *Sky Queen* on its return flight from Detroit. He had imitated Wyvern's voice, using the pet name "Carrottop" which he had heard Wyvern call his daughter.

Kimer had also broadcast the mysterious radio threat when Tom was flying home from the Pentagon. Afterward, he and his henchmen had tried to kill Tom or frighten him out of going on with his Silentenna project by driving past the Swifts' home at night and firing the sonic weapon which had caused Tom to black out.

Gammon had also managed to sabotage the trim-control system of the jet, in the hope that Tom might pilot the plane and crash.

"I still don't see why you had Fronz substitute dummy crystals in my first Silentenna."

Kimer chuckled. "If the demonstration failed and you were made to look like a fool, I thought there was less chance the government would use your device to stop our sonic attacks."

Tom racked his brain for some way to keep his enemy talking. "What do you intend to do now?"

"I intend to make sure that you two can never give us away. Then we can at least sell our sonic blitz devices to some foreign power."

Kimer's eyes narrowed as he went on, "There is, of course, the possibility of a deal—if you'd swear to keep your mouth shut and put your scientific skill at my disposal."

"Not a chance!" Tom said scornfully.

Kimer gave a vicious laugh. "Then your bodies will be found in due time without a mark on them to show what happened."

Turning to his two henchmen, Kimer added, "Find their aircraft and get it out of sight quickly. I'll attend to Swift and his friend."

Again Kimer chuckled. "It should afford me a splendid opportunity for scientific observation and note-taking! And you, Swift, will now have a chance to learn firsthand the horrible effects of noise stress. My guess is that you will survive not more than twenty minutes."

As Gammon and Fronz hurried off, Kimer slammed and latched the door of the sonic test cell. Tom whispered a few hasty words to Bud.

Then the sound was turned on—a low shriek that gradually swelled to a shattering blast. The cell seemed to explode with noise!

Kimer peered through the quartz-glass window. His grin changed to a furious scowl.

The two boys were lounging casually against the wall, smiling and chatting!

Kimer angrily checked his control switches. Still the boys appeared totally unconcerned.

"What's wrong?" Kimer wondered. "Isn't the sound on in there—or is Swift protecting them with some sort of concealed equipment?"

Kimer opened the door. A torrent of sound came blasting out. Puzzled and furious, he rushed into the cell to search Tom Swift.

But a leg was suddenly thrust in his way. Kimer tripped and cursed. Before he could lash out, Bud gave him a kick that sent him sprawling forward! Kimer's head struck the wall with stunning force, knocking him unconscious!

Bud stood over him, ready to kick again at the first sign of movement. Tom hurried out of the cell and turned off the sound by pressing the switches with his elbow.

Bud gasped with relief. "Whew! I can hardly see

straight! Another minute of pretending I didn't hear that noise and I'd have gone nuts!"

"It was our only hope of outwitting Kimer," Tom said. "I was a near-stretcher case, myself!"

Tom found a hacksaw among the tools in the room and cut his wrist bonds by rubbing them against the blade. Then he untied Bud.

"What next, pal?" the young copilot asked when they had trussed Kimer.

Tom glanced at the control board. "There's a radio transceiver over there. Enterprises was tracking our Duck or radar, so help should be on the way. But I'll hurry them up with a call."

Tom soon contacted George Dilling, the Swifts' radio chief. As he finished talking, the boys heard steps in the laboratory overhead.

"Gammon and Fronz are coming!" Tom hissed. "Quick! Duck down behind those tool bins!"

Tom let out a harsh, muffled yell for help. Then he, too, dropped out of sight.

Steps came dashing down the stairway. Finding the control room apparently empty, Fronz and Gammon rushed toward the sonic cell.

"Kimer's in there, but the kids are gone!" Fronz exclaimed.

The two engineers darted into the cell to release their boss. Tom and Bud popped from their hiding places as if shot from a catapult. In an instant the cell door was slammed and latched, trapping their three foes inside!

Bud exploded in laughter as he saw Fronz and Gammon roaring with fury inside. Kimer was just reviving dizzily.

"Less noise in there," Bud shouted, "or we may have to drown you out with a sonic blast!"

Minutes later, the *Sky Queen* was hovering down over the building, now ablaze with light. Mr. Swift, Ames, Norris and two other FBI men soon landed. They grinned admiringly as Tom and Bud showed their prisoners.

"Nice work, fellows," said Norris. "Interpol just notified us that the last member of the Delpertas' gang has been caught."

"And John Wyvern is almost himself again, Tom," Mr. Swift added. "He recognizes Elsa and his memory is coming back."

"That's great, Dad!"

Bud clapped his friend on the back. "Well, pal, I suppose you have another big project in mind?"

Tom's eyes twinkled. "As a matter of fact, I'd like to do some research in *infra*sonics."

But a thrilling and unexpected adventure would soon lead Tom to invent his *Subocean Geotron*.

With a groan of mock dismay, Bud said, "What! More sound? After you've just silenced any sonic attackers forever!"

Tom merely grinned.